# Hardy's Redemption

Eric Kubat

# NOTE FROM AUTHOR

While the location and characters of this story were created in the author's mind and are not a real place or real people; the thoughts, feelings, emotions experienced, and general reactions to those are very real. Those who provide public safety services can relate to these characters and may be able to see themselves or those they work with in these characters. Family and friends will also be able to see their loved ones these characters.

This book is intended for an adult audience as it talks about Post Traumatic Stress, Moral Injury, and the struggle that many public safety professionals face while trying to manage the symptoms of these while trying to live a "normal" life. I put normal in quotes because many of us in public safety questions what is normal. We see the absolute best of society, as well as the very worst. Often, we see both in the same shift, or within a few hours or minutes. The emotional whiplash and adrenaline roller coaster can be both physically and mentally exhausting.

For my brothers and sisters in public safety, your dedication is appreciated. If you are struggling with the difficulties of this profession, you are not alone! Please reach out to someone, it could be a family member, friend, religious leader, mental health professional, or a combination of these. The point is to reach out. You are not weak, you are human.

If you are a family or friend of someone in public safety, I hope this story helps you understand a little better what is in our heads at times and may explain why we are the way we are after a shift. This is not us asking for a free pass, but better understanding may help guide conversations and discussions. This profession is rewarding and purposeful, however, it can come with a significant physical and emotional cost.

Thank you for reading this story. This is planned to be a five-book series following the Blue River Fire Protection district and the main characters as they develop and grow, both personally and professionally.

# CONTENTS

# ACKNOWLEDGMENTS

I would like to thank my wife, Stephanie, for her love, grace, and understanding. Being married to someone who works in public safety cannot be easy. I appreciate everything you have done and continue to do for our children and myself.

I would like to thank my children, Caitlin, Haley and Ethan. I am proud to be your father, and I am excited to watch you grow and learn.

Thank you to Audrey Beitler for the cover design. Please see her website www.audreybeitler.com for a sample of her work.

Thank you to Jill Lee for her content editing. I appreciate all your thoughts and opinions about story flow and character development.

Thank you to Rochelle Hawthorne for our discussions on mental health in public safety. Thank you for continuing to advocate for mental wellness, even in retirement.

Thank you to Emily Kubat and Wendy Mainka for agreeing to be beta readers. Your opinions and thoughts will also help this series develop and tell a better story.

Lastly, thank YOU readers for giving this book a chance and letting this story be told. I appreciate every single one of you. Could you please leave a review wherever you bought a copy of this book? Feedback is crucial and will help me become a better storyteller.

1

"This is your fault! You should have been there to save us!" A familiar voice screams through the dense fog.

"I'm sorry!" I hear myself reply. My voice is so quiet I wonder if I replied aloud, or if it was just in my head.

"I failed you…and Wilma… and Theo." I continue through a sobbing choke. Tears flowing down my face faster than the rapids of the Blue River that runs through town. My throat is wet and constricted, yet feeling as gritty and rough as the Sahara Desert.

"I will never forgive myself. I promise!" I finish with a voice that fades away slowly into the receding fog. A loud crash reverberates through my head so forcefully that I can't help but fall to the ground in a fetal position and cover my ears. My head feels as if there are half a dozen miners trapped in there, trying to dig out with pickaxes.

My eyes pop open as I vault up into a sitting position in a bed. It takes a few seconds to shake the fog away as I slowly become aware of my surroundings. My senses slowly come back one by one. I feel cold and wet. I shiver as I feel around and find my fleece bedsheets and pillow drenched. My hair is plastered to my scalp, and my skin has a slick sheen to it.

A loud "Crash" that reminds me of an exceptionally large monkey smashing cymbals together, redirects my attention to the window where I notice for the first time, there is a very powerful thunderstorm taking out its fury in a wrathful vengeance. Another crash caused my window and window frame to shake violently.

I can smell the electricity in the air with a burning undertone as I start to taste the saltiness of my sweat on my lips. With all of my senses returning, I walk over to the window and see a tree in the yard smoldering with fractured limbs and charred bark lying on the ground. Rain pelts the window with wave after wave, whipped by the wind. I find it fitting as the realization hits me…. It happened again. My mood instantly matches the raging wrath outside. I glance at the clock. The fiery red 4:04am tauntingly stares back at me with a smugness that throws me further down the depression rabbit hole.

I mentally throw out my hands and feet in an attempt to stop this downward slide into depression. My therapist came up with this trick; to help me not only recognize the slide, but also help stop or slow the slide. At first, I was skeptical and laughed. Honestly, it has helped me on more than one occasion. Taking some deep breaths while square breathing, I feel the descent into the abyss gradually slow and come to a stop. I like the square breathing technique. That is where you take a big slow deep breath over a span of five seconds, hold your breath for five seconds, breathe out slowly over 5 seconds emptying your lungs, hold your breath for 5 seconds, and repeat.

With my heart rate under control, and my sense of bearing more focused, I get to work stripping my bedding off the bed and pillows to start the ritual of cleansing my sheets of the evidence of another nightmare. It has been a month since my last nightmare, and honestly, I am caught by surprise. The right side, or logical side of my brain, says the thunderstorm raging outside triggered the nightmare. The left side, or emotional side of my brain, argues that they have been on my mind recently and that trip down memory lane cost me dearly. I stifle a chuckle as it feels like I have the devil on one shoulder arguing with the angel on the other shoulder. The visual image popping into my head has me laughing out loud.

"Oh man, I really am a mess right now" I say out loud to my empty house as I carry the sheets to the laundry room. With the bedding in the wash, I meander down the hall to the kitchen to start brewing the bitter nectar of life I need and crave…. Coffee. I turn on the under-cabinet lights that illuminate the kitchen in a soft glow and hit the power button for the TV. As I open the bag of coffee and inhale the rich aroma of my favorite dark roast, I hear the meteorologist announce the worst of the storm is passing through, but it will continue to rain until midafternoon. With coffee dripping into the carafe, I review the work schedule for today. Looks like I will not be working today, as we had a large flower garden remodel on the schedule.

"Thank you, mother nature," I mumble sarcastically to the empty room.

I pour my first cup of coffee, take a slow, savoring sip and head back to the bathroom to shower the last remaining remnant of my nightmare away. I stand under the pulsating shower jet as it kneads my shoulders and back, releasing a tension I did not realize I had. Feeling even better, I lather up, rinse off and step out of the shower. Dried and dressed, I walked out to the front door and grab the newspaper. Yes, I still subscribe to a physical newspaper. Call me old fashioned if you will, but I love the feel of the paper in my hands while I read the current news.

I make my breakfast of vanilla yogurt with a drizzle of honey and a banana. I am not really the breakfast type, but I know I need to eat something to fuel my body for the day. I sit down at the table and relax. This is my favorite part of the day; good coffee and my newspaper. My little slice of heaven. I open the paper, savor another sip of coffee and dive in. Unable to focus, I read and re-read the same paragraph over and over again. My mind continues its journey down memory lane, a lane I really don't like going down. They flash through my mind again bringing with it pain, sadness, and anger. Anger at the universe, and anger at myself. The chirp of my cell phone breaks me free. I look at my phone, and it is Manny, my boss telling me what I already figured, the job scheduled for today is postponed due to the rain.

With my day quickly unraveling, I feel the walls closing in. That's the thing with loss, depression, and self-punishment; it does not take much to throw you in a tailspin. I need to get out of the house and discharge some of this pent-up tension and clear my head. I see on the radar, the thunder and lightning have safely passed, and it is just a light to moderate rain. I change into my moisture, wicking running clothes and Brooks running shoes. A good run seems to do the trick, and I feel a good run in the rain is just what I need.

I stretch out my muscles, trying to warm them up while I debate running my short loop, normal loop, or my long loop. I decide to start running and see where it takes me. I take off at a comfortable 9 minute a mile pace and run north through the neighborhood and out to Blue River Parkway and head toward the business district. As the minutes and miles pass by, I feel the tension start to leave. I pass by the unique building designed and occupied by Structural Designs Architectural Group. Its unique design with sharp angles, steel, and glass exterior just begs to be noticed by anyone passing by. What a great marketing strategy I think to myself. I pass by a few more businesses and then loop back towards home. I arrived back home an hour and a half after I left, concluding my ten-mile run, feeling the burning of my lungs and muscles. I guess it was the long route, not that it was truly up for debate. The run not only cleared my tension, but it also cleared my mind. First, off to shower for the second time today, then make a phone call. Hopefully, there is room in the schedule for me today.

I pick up my phone and hit the contact button for Sheila. It rings twice before she answers.

"Hello Hardy, it's kind of early in the morning. Are you Ok?" She answers her phone with apprehension in her voice.

"Hey Sheila, do you have room today in your schedule for me?" I ask, glancing at the clock and just now realizing it is only 7am.

"It sounds like you are bogged down with something. Let me check my schedule.  I have an opening at noon. How does that work for you? Or does it need to be sooner? "She replies then pauses.  "Hardy, are you thinking of harming yourself or others?"  She finishes with her voice sounding more alert and concerned, waiting for my answer.

"Noon works for me.  No work today thanks to the rain.  No, I am not going to self-harm or hurt others, I just finished a run and am feeling better.  But….. I had another one and it … well, it has taken me by surprise and has put me off kilter….."  I reply trailing off at the end.

"And…. I want to discuss something big with you.  I was going to wait until our next session but today seems like a good time as any"  I finish with as much indifference as I can muster.

"Ok, I will see you at noon.  It was good to hear from you; I am glad you called".  She replies with a cheerful lit to her voice.  With that phone call completed, I grab my coffee, paper, and head to my covered front porch to try and relax with the lulling rainfall and my creature comforts of newspaper and coffee.

Sheila lives a few minutes outside of town on 5 acres of land.  She owns her own therapy clinic and built a small office on her land.  The clinic is nestled in the woods away from the bustle and sounds of the city.  A natural creek meanders by and during the times I have been out here, I have spotted deer, wild turkey, and many smaller animals.  The entire setting does a very good job of relaxing people.  I walk in the door and hear the bell jingle.  Not an electronic doorbell, but a good old-fashioned gold bell that gets bumped and chimes when the door is opened.

"Good afternoon, Hardy" Sheila calls out as she smiles at me. I am not sure how she does it, but she has this natural smile that puts you at ease and compels a person to open up.

"So, you had the dream again? If you don't mind, walk me through it" she starts the conversation as she studies me intently.

"Well, first the fog appears, or maybe it looks like fog but is really smoke. I don't know, it doesn't smell like smoke, but it is the same thing all the time. She is yelling at me that it is all my fault and that I should have been there to save them. And then I say I am sorry, that I failed her, Wilma, and Theo. Finally, I say I will never forgive myself, I promise. Then I woke up drenched in sweat. Although this time a loud cymbal like crashing sound tore through my head in the dream. When I woke up, a thunderstorm was passing through." I say this in one big, long rush, barely coming up for air.

"It has been...what...a month, month and a half since your last one? Do you have any thoughts on what may have brought it on?" She presses me with a knowing look. She's good, really good. There is something I haven't told her yet.

"Well, I feel like I am gaining back control of my life. The landscaping job is fun, but I just don't feel... I don't know how to explain it. I just don't feel a sense of purpose, or it feels like a part of me is colored gray. I miss my old job, and I want to get back into that line of work." Saying it out loud to someone else feels like a burden has been lifted off my chest.

"But you feel like these dreams are telling you no?" I nod, unable to speak. Like I said, she is really good. It is almost scary how she can read people and connect with them.

"You were a paramedic for Lime County EMS when the fire occurred, correct? Is that where you want to go"

"Not exactly, I have applied for and have been accepted into the next academy for the Blue River Fire Protection District as a firefighter/paramedic.  I start in two weeks" I can't keep the smile off my face as I grin at Sheila

"Well, congratulations Hardy! This is a huge step.  What do you say we meet every Friday after the academy is done for the week and check in?  Does that sound good to you? "

"That sounds great to me.  Thank you, Sheila, for everything you have helped me through.  I don't know where I would be, or what I would be if it weren't for your help".

I walk out of the clinic with a sense of calm washing over me and a new resolve that I am making the right choice.  As I head to my vehicle, I call my landscaping boss to give him my two-week notice.  His answer surprised me.  He laughs, says about damn time, although he is going to miss working with me.  He ends the call saying that is where I belong, not digging in dirt all day long.

2

I pulled into the parking lot at 0700 hours. The academy starts at 0800 but I need a few minutes to steel my nerves, collect my thoughts and convince myself I made the right decision. I look out and see the classroom building, the class A burn building, the class B burn building, several fire trucks, an ambulance, a 5-story tower, and a very large concrete pad. There are several people walking around with purpose. One of them looks familiar. I close my eyes and listen to the radio. Brooks and Dunn "Brand new Man" is playing, and I sing along. I let the sound of their voices, and the steel guitar warm over me. Feeling committed, I step out of my truck, grab my lunch box, backpack, and head to the front doors of the classroom building.

I take a seat and look around at the 7 other recruits in the class. They all look like kids, and suddenly I feel very out of place. I have some

9

patches of grey in my hair, crow's feet around my eyes, and big puffy bags under my eyes. Stress wreaks havoc on the body. As much as I work out to relieve that stress, I try to keep my weight and waist size within the normal measurements for my height. It takes considerably more effort than it did 10 years ago. There is nothing I can do about the grey hair and crows feet. I refuse to dye my hair, and I really don't laugh or smile much anymore, so the crows feet are not as noticeable. Even though we are different ages, we wear the same uniform of black boots, navy blue pants, and navy-blue t-shirt with our first initial and last name screen printed on both the front and back. It is a standard issue academy uniform.

The training cadre enters, and we all jump to stand at attention. The three of them walk to the front of the room and stand there for a very long moment, staring at us. It is unnerving, I feel like a lab specimen under a microscope. Their eyes are cold, clinical. No smile on their face as their eyes roam over each one of us.

"Good morning, Recruit class 20-02" says a sharply dressed petite female wearing deputy chief collar brass. Her presence is commanding and demands attention. She has a voice and posture that pours out confidence and competence.

"Good morning, Deputy Chief" replies the class in unison.

"I am Deputy Chief Jill Delaney." She says with a commanding voice. "I am responsible for the implementation of standards and training for the Blue River Fire Protection District. This academy will challenge you both mentally and physically. It is not going to be easy. We have high standards and expect you to exceed them. While nobody's perfect, we expect you to work hard, learn, build on your skills, teamwork, and improve every day. That learning and improvement does not end at the conclusion of this academy. That is the expectation for as long as you are a member of this organization. If you do not agree with this, there is the door, and you can leave now." silence ensues as she stares at each and every one of us. It is silent for so long, it gives us all time to second guess being here. No one moves or makes a sound.

"Next to me is Capt. James Everett. He is the staff training captain." Capt. Everett stares at us and nods his head ever so slightly.

"Next to him is Capt. Sal Domingo. He is the Engine 2 Captain on C shift. He is assisting Capt. Everett for this recruit class." Capt. Domingo stares at us like a stone statue. His face rock hard and horseshoe mustache with not a hair out of place. This is the guy that looks so familiar. I still can't place him. How do I know him, I ask myself. And with that, Deputy Chief Delaney walks out of the building.

"Recruit Class 20-02. Line up outside. PT time." Barks Capt. Everett. Everyone jumps up and files out in a single line moving with purpose. Day one PT holds nothing back. We spent an hour and a half completing a circuit loop of running one mile, 10 kettlebell swings, finishing with the stair climb to the top of the tower and back down. When that loop is finished, we start all over again. That was brutal. I have my hands behind my head trying to expand my chest as large as possible to draw in as much air as I can.

My eyes are closed as I take deep breaths when I hear "You're not going to die on us old man, are you?" with a hint of a smile in the voice. I turn around and see recruit Whitman smiling at me like he just told the world's funniest joke.

"I kept up with you, didn't I?" I shoot back with a smile on my face. An honest to God smile. It felt good. No, that isn't right…. It felt great.

I look at our group and see everyone looking a little tired but smiling and cheering everyone on. I look over and I swear I see a hint of a smile on the Cadres' faces, even if it was only for a fraction of a second. "Ok, enough fun. Back to the classroom" Barks Capt. Everett.

Back in the classroom we go over the Blue River Fire Protection structure, staffing and response area. We learn that Blue River, Wyoming is a growing city. The population at the last census was 75,000. The Blue River Fire Protection District is a 5 station, 145 uniformed personnel department. They staff 5 fire engines, 3 ladder trucks, 1 heavy rescue, 1 hazmat squad and 2 Battalion Chiefs. The administrative staff includes 1 fire chief, two deputy chiefs. One is responsible for operations, and the other is responsible for standards and training. There is also a fire marshal who supervises two inspectors/fire investigators, as well as a plans examiner. The fire protection district covers all of Blue River, plus 4 surrounding rural townships and 75 square miles of unincorporated area. The main employer in the city is the chemical manufacturing plant Chemical Development Incorporated.

We break for lunch and chat among ourselves as the training captains disappear. I'm sure they are talking about how we are doing so far. I find out that Lisa is a third-generation firefighter, and this is all she has ever wanted to do.

Derrick used to be a police officer, and while he liked law

enforcement, he liked the 24-hour shift structure which allows him to have more quality time at home with his wife and young family. His wife also liked that he would be working in a crew instead of out on patrol of desolate country roads by himself where backup could easily be 30 minutes away.

John is the first in his family to not follow the footsteps into the family ranching business. While he doesn't mind helping out,  he wanted to do something more fulfilling.

Meredith is an adrenaline junkie and laughs as she explains how she needs a high adrenaline job to keep her occupied between her backcountry skiing, cave diving, and skydiving adventures.

Dan is a little more reserved and states he applied when he saw how the firefighters treated his neighbors after they lost their home to a fire.  He said they were compassionate, explained next steps to move forward, and were able to save several irreplaceable items that were mementos of their deceased infant son. He finished by saying this is an organization I want to work for.

Tyler and Joey went to high school together.  They have been best friends since kindergarten and have been inseparable since.  They think this job will help them get more dates.  They are a little immature in my opinion but then again who wasn't at 21 and 22 years old.  I can tell they are good kids.  They just need a little mentoring and guidance.

I have been silent until now.  With that, everyone looks at me expectantly.  I struggle with what to tell them.  I have an ugly past, and I really don't know them well enough to bare my soul.  So, I take the easy way out and say I was in landscaping and looking for a career change. It really wasn't a lie, I was in landscaping, and I have never worked as a firefighter before. But it also wasn't the full truth either.

After lunch we are fitted with turnout gear and SCBA mask. The turnout gear consists of jacket, pants, boots, gloves, nomex hood, and helmet. Once we find gear that fits, we head back into the classroom for a death by PowerPoint lecture on how BRFP uses the minute man load on all crosslay lines.

We learn how to load it in the hose bed and how to deploy it by placing the nozzle and first coupling at the point of entry. We learn about the skid load off the back of the truck. That is 600 ft of 2.5 inch hose in a flat load towards the back of the hose bed with an additional forward 200 ft stacked in four 50 foot sections with graduated loops for easy deployment. Attached to the end of that is 100 ft of 1 ¾ inch hose bundled together. This is used for long setback homes or our 3 and 4 floor apartments that do not have standpipes in the stairwells to use. Think of the 2.5 inch hose as a horizontal standpipe in these scenarios.

My head is spinning by the end of the lectures. We have a short break then end the day with a lecture on the use and maintenance of our SCBAs.

The day is over, and I am exhausted. My brain hurts from information overload. I head home, make a monster deli sandwich, a couple of dill pickle spears, drink about a gallon of water and slip off to bed.

The first week passes by in much the same way the first day did. We have morning PT which continues to push us or punish us, if you will. Although, the punishment is self-inflicted as we continue to push each other and make a friendly competition out of it. I do notice our group becoming more cohesive as we push, challenge, and encourage each other. I can see the mindset start to change from "me" to "we".

The afternoons are spent in the classroom learning about the different hose we carry, what the hose diameters mean, how many gallons per minute we can flow through the various hoses, and different nozzles, smooth bore versus fog nozzles. We learned that nozzle use is department specific and here, we use smooth bore on our preconnected cross lays and fog nozzles on our bumper line. We also talked about search techniques and crew integrity. We talked about matching our search with the probable structure layout.

We talked about looking at a building and identifying the most probable location for the kitchen and bedrooms. Crew integrity was pounded into our heads over and over again. We must maintain contact with our crew using sight, sound, or touch at all times depending on the condition and visibility of the atmosphere we are entering.

Week one is complete, we are all looking forward to our weekend and a much-needed break from all the lecturers and classroom lessons. Next week, we will be hands-on in the buildings practicing the theories we have learned.

Feeling a renewed energy and enthusiasm, I head off to check in with Sheila, then I am going to treat myself with a dinner consisting of a mushroom Swiss burger, steak fries and the largest glass of ice-cold sweet tea I can get my hands on. I used to enjoy a cold beer or bourbon occasionally, but after the fire, it became a needed crutch to dull the pain. It took a while and a lot of effort to stop that downward spiral into the bottom of the bottle. I don't trust myself to even crack that door open at this time.

I park in front of the office and step out. I walk to the front door and open it. I hear the familiar ringing of the bell and smile. Sheila looks up from her computer, "Hello Hardy, ready to start?" she says as she smiles warmly.

"let's do this" I reply, unable to keep the smile spreading across my face.

I talk about the first week and my apprehension the first morning. I continue with how that apprehension has faded away and excitement has taken its place. We talk about the other recruits and how different we all are, yet we are working together towards a common goal. In just one week we have gone from strangers to building friendships that maybe could be sustained. She listens with the attention of a hawk soaring over a field looking for a meal. 'Why did you phrase it that way?' she asks. I look at her with my eyebrows scrunched down in confusion. "Phrase what in what way? I ask in return. "You said building friendships that maybe could be sustained." I think back to what I said, and I didn't even realize I had phrased it that way.

I explain to her that while I get along with everyone, and feel friendships forming, I am hesitant to open up and talk about anything before being a landscaper. As far as the other recruits know, I am a landscaper that wanted a career change.

"Why is that?" She challenges me while staring me down.

"Because they are young, and starry eyed about the job and I don't want to dim the fire burning in their eyes." I lie while avoiding eye contact. The real reason is I don't want to open up to anyone ever again.

It is too painful. To open up is inviting the eventual heartbreak that will happen. I don't think I would survive round two. It is divine intervention that I survived round one this long. She knows my answer is a bullshit copout, but she doesn't push me to keep discussing it. She does something worse…. She gives me homework.

"I want you to think about the other recruits and what they bring to the group. They may be young; however, everyone brings something to contribute. By not being open and honest, is that contributing to the group, or taking away from the growth of the group?".

I trust Sheila, she is the only one I truly trust and it was a long, hard, winding road that doubled back more times than I can count to get there. I don't know if I have the energy to travel that road again. One thing's for sure; that question will be on my mind all weekend.

I pull into the Silver Spur bar and grill for my promised burger and tea. The Silver Spur has the best burgers in the state. It is clear I'm not the only one with that opinion, as the parking lot is packed. I check in at the hostess stand and there are no tables available but there is a spot at the bar. I don't want to sit at the bar…. too tempting. I also don't want to wait because I am hungry and tired. I stand there having this mental debate in my head while the hostess stares at me waiting for my decision.

I really want this burger, and I don't want to wait. "I will sit at the bar". I reply quietly to her. I follow her to the bar and sit down. The bartender saunters up and places a napkin on the bar in front of me. "What can I get you?" he says while looking at the beers on tap.

"Mushroom Swiss burger, steak fries, and an extra-large sweet tea." I rush out in one breath before I can change my mind while staring at the beers on tap. "Please and thank you" I add and the end mentally chastising myself for the lack of manners. My mom didn't raise me that way.

A few minutes later he sets my sweet tea down in front of me. I take a long, deep pull and savor the sweet cool liquid as it slides down my throat. I look around and take in my surroundings. There is a cover band playing all my favorite country hits from Brooks and Dunn, Garth Brooks, Alan Jackson, Chris LeDoux, and George Strait, among others. I see couples two stepping to the songs and for a moment it makes me miss a life I will never have again.

The pain is too much; I look away and stare at the back of the bar. I am jolted out of my thoughts when the bartender sets my burger and fries in front of me.

"Is there anything else I can get for you?" he asks quickly as others call for his attention.

I quickly glance at my fantastic looking meal and tell him no. He rushes off to fill more drink orders. I look at the burger for a moment and take in the perfectly melted Swiss over the glistening sauteed mushrooms on a soft and warm pretzel bun. The steak fries are plentiful with a perfect golden crispness to them. I take another pull off the sweet tea and grab the burger. The first bite is heaven as the flavors and textures blend together. Like I said, the best burgers in the state.

I take my time savoring the meal and tea while listening to the music. With my meal finished, the bartender returns to clear my plate.

"Another one?" he asks while nodding to my empty glass of

sweet tea.

Oh, why not, I think to myself. "Yes please" I reply.

I burned enough calories this week to splurge. I sit at the bar, drinking my sweet tea and listening to the music. I feel content. It is a foreign feeling to me. I just can't help the smile that spreads across my face.

While the band plays "Little Man" by Alan Jackson, I feel a tap on my shoulder. I turn and see Whitman standing there.

"Hey Whitman, how are you?" I say with surprise in my voice.

"I'm good. The whole gang is sitting over at that table. Come over and join us" he says while pointing at a long table with a dozen people sitting at it. "We have been calling your name for the last 15 minutes, but I guess the music is too loud for your old ears to hear" he continues with a smirking grin.

I stare for a long moment and see the drinks flowing, along with laughter and shenanigans. Several of the others are waving at me to join them. My heart rate starts to speed up, my palms are sweating, and oh my, did someone turn the heat up?

"I'm sorry Whitman, I was just getting ready to leave. I'm tired and have a long day tomorrow. I appreciate the offer, but I am going to have to decline this time" I am lying through my teeth and hope he is not able to see through it.

He stares at me for what feels like forever but in reality, was probably seconds. I can tell he is debating if he should call me on my lie. His mind made up, he claps me on the back and tells me he expects me to join the group next Friday as he walks back to the table with his arms out and palms up while shaking his head.

I feel bad but I just can't.  Forming connections only leads to heartbreak.  That has been my lifesaver for these last several years.

I signal to the bartender that I am ready for my bill.  I pay my bill and head out to my truck.  The cool night air washes over me and settles my nerves.  I sit in my truck for a moment and stare into space, thinking over the words Sheila asked me.  I almost get out of my truck and walk back, instead I start the truck and drive home.

The weekend flies by in a blur as I stay busy with cleaning and maintaining my house.  My house is never really dirty, but I like things clean and organized. I also go for several long runs.  Running helps me think through issues that are on my mind.  I put my earbuds in, set a comfortable pace and have an internal monologue debating what is on my mind.  Feeling a sense of accomplishment, I sit down Sunday evening with a good book and read for a solid 3 hours before I head to bed.  The start of academy week two is set to begin.

Week two begins in much the same fashion as Week one.  All the recruits return with smiles on their faces.  We are ready for the challenge of putting into practice the theories and skills we have learned about in the classroom.

"Good morning recruit class 20-02."  Barks Capt. Everett.

"Good morning, Sir!" the group replies with spirit.

The PT session this morning is brutal.  We stair climb while wearing full turnout gear and SCBA harness.  If that wasn't enough, we also have to carry a 50fft section of 2 ½ inch hose.  We walk to the top level, turn around and walk back down.  Once at the bottom, we head to the Keiser sled to simulate forcing entry, then we go to the third station and used  a New York Hook on the ceiling prop for two minutes.  The ceiling prop is a device that mimics the action of pulling sheetrock or similar material from a ceiling while checking for fire extension or hidden fire.  Once that circuit is done, we start over.  By the end of PT, my arms and legs feel like Jello.

I look around and see I am not the only one who is feeling the effects of the grueling PT session.  Dan looks like he is going to pass out.  He is sitting on the stairs bent over at the waist.  Meredith is lying out on her back chest rising and falling at a rapid pace.  Tyler and Joey were slowly walking around shaking out their arms and legs while looking around.

For the next 2 hours we load, deploy, then reload and re-deploy the minuteman load. We are required to place the loops in the correct places and at the correct lengths.  If it is not correct, we will have to start over. The goal is to load it correctly every time and deploy it flawlessly. If we make even one mistake loading and deploying, we will do it again. The constant repetition turned us into machines.  By the end of the session, our bodies are moving on auto pilot, and we are loading and deploying the hose lines without much thought at all.

Lunch passes by with minimal talking.  I think people are still recovering from all the activity this morning.  That afternoon, we spend the time practicing our search techniques. We practice with and without a hose line. We learn how to navigate stairs safely.  We even use smoke machines to get the buildings to as near zero visibility as possible.  It is a long, exhausting day. When I arrive home, I make a sandwich, shower, and promptly fell asleep.

The rest of the week is much the same as the first day of week 2. We have challenging PT sessions in the morning with more hands-on practical exercises on the skills we have learned. While we were working together as a team, something felt off.

The other recruits would talk and joke among themselves, then go quiet when I approached. It felt like I was being excluded from something. No one would say anything bad; however, the atmosphere was different. It appeared the training cadre also noticed as they continued to talk about the importance of teamwork and bonding. They would bring up the old cliche that at times, the life of the crew may depend on me doing my job correctly at the correct time and vice versa. I made the decision to join the group on Friday evening and make an appearance.

I had been thinking about Sheila and her comments on group dynamics all week. The odd feeling and behavior of the other recruits causes my mind to go into overdrive as I analyze the week. I hope I am not the cause of the tension. That is how I justify my decision to go. I don't want to talk about my past; however, I also don't want to be the cause of tension during the academy.

Friday during our lunch break, I ask Joey where everyone is meeting tonight. The room goes silent, and everyone stares at Joey. That 15 seconds just confirmed my suspicion. I am the cause of the tension. I take this opportunity to try and mend some bridges that I clearly burned last week by declining to join them.

"It is clear I disappointed you all last week by not joining you at the Silver Spur. I apologize for declining the invitation. I won't make excuses for it. Can we try again?" I say with as much courage as I can muster while trying to look at everyone in the group.

There is a pause long enough that I swear the Earth stopped spinning. I then see a couple people nod approval, and I hear the Silver Spur 7pm thrown out.

When the academy ends for the week, I make my way to meet Sheila. My mood is morose, and I am so lost in thought that I almost miss my turn into her driveway. I open the door and the bell chimes. It feels like a gong in my head. Sheila looks up from her computer, and her eyes go soft. "Rough week Hardy?"

"I screwed up by not joining the group Friday night and it is causing friction" I say as the honesty in the statement just pours out. I take a seat and stare at the wall for a long moment.

"Tell me more about that and why you declined the invitation." She says as she relaxes into her chair readying herself to listen intently.

"Well, I went to the Silver Spur for my burger and tea after our meeting last week. I did not know the group was getting together that night. Joey came up and tapped me on the shoulder and said the group was sitting at a table and asked me to join them. When I looked over and saw them laughing and joking with each other and what I assume were some girlfriends/boyfriends/spouses, I felt a panic attack coming on. I declined and said I had places to be and promptly left."

"Why didn't you explain to him why you felt like you couldn't join the group? This is what we talked about last week. Taking this job is a huge step towards building yourself back up. Hiding your feelings and needs, however, is only going to weaken the bond that you need with your crew members to perform your job effectively and safely. If they feel you aren't being honest and truthful, it takes away from that trust. You may not have been a firefighter, but I can venture a guess that those same principles apply in EMS."

I hang my head as I let those words sink in to me. I know she is right. How am I going to do this job if I keep everyone at arm's length. When I really think about it, that is the reason I left Lime County EMS. "You are right Sheila. I just don't know how to do it. I panic and take the easy way out." I speak.

"Start by being honest when asked a question. For instance, if one of the group asks about your family, tell them the truth. If you're not ready to talk about it, you could say that talking about family is difficult and you are not ready to talk about your family yet. You can explain you have suffered a significant loss and talking about it brings that loss back." The understanding in her eyes is reassuring.

"I want to be able to talk about them. It just hurts too much." Moisture starts pooling in my eyes.

"You will get there Hardy. You stating that you want to, is evidence of that. Six months ago, you would not have said that. You are working your way through the grieving process. There is no timeframe for that process. Everyone moves through it at a different pace. It can be very uncomfortable, I know you can do it. I think you are ready. Remember, it took you a while to be open and honest with me. The hardest part is starting. Take that first step." Her eyes seem to glow as the truth of her words sink into me.

We have a very platonic relationship, yet I have opened up to her. I take a deep breath as a sense of calm comes over me as I realize I have already taken that first step to speaking about them without even realizing it. I leave the check in session with a renewed energy as I head over to the Silver Spur.

The parking lot is packed as I circle the lot and find a place to park. The 80s and 90s country hits are audible from the door as people come and go. I make my way to the door, and I feel someone walking next to me. I glance to my right and see a woman about five foot five inches tall, wearing slacks, a blouse, and a blazer that fits her form perfectly. As nice as the clothes look on her, it was her hair and eyes that made me catch my breath. Her hair was a mix of red and brown that seemed to change color as the strands moved in the light. Her eyes were the brightest emerald green I have ever seen. She seemed to have this glow around her that just drew me in.

Without even thinking, I opened the door and held it open for her. As she walked by, the music seemed to fade away and all I heard was the soft thank you that flowed over me. It felt like those two words had wrapped itself around me in a hug. The moment was over just as fast as it arrived, and I heard the music and chatter of the bar along with some guy yelling "Hey Dylan, we are over here!" The woman looks towards the direction of the voice, gives a wave and makes her way over. I never would have guessed her as a Dylan, I think to myself as I look for my academy mates.

I spot the group sitting at a long picnic table with wooden benches. I make my way through the crowd and see Joey look up and a smile spread across his face.

"Hey Hardy, we are glad you could make it." He looks over across the bar and nods his head, "who is the lady you walked in with?"

"I didn't come with anyone." I reply as I look at him confused.

"You walked in with a woman wearing dress clothes. You both just stood there with the door open staring at each other like you were the only two here. Who is she? asked Meredith.

"I don't know who she is. We just walked up to the door together. I held the door open for her. I don't know her." I reply as I sit down shaking my head wondering what punch line of a joke I am missing.

The waiter comes over, and I order a sweet tea and a mushroom Swiss burger with steak fries. I turn my attention back to the group as I am introduced to all the spouses and significant others.

"Hey guys, sorry I'm late. There were a couple things I needed to finish up for the last proposal." Dylan says as she joins her group.

"Who was that guy you walked in with?" Rick asks, eyebrows raised as he nods to the door.

"What guy? I came here right from the office; I didn't bring anyone." Dylan says with confusion on her face.

"That guy you were staring at in the front door. You both were both looking at each other as if you had found what you were looking for." adds Adam. "It was the weirdest thing to see".

"I have never met him before. He held the door open for me, and I said thank you." Dylan says while shaking her head. "Enough about me, let's celebrate securing the latest contract and for the continued success of Structural Designs Architectural Group."

Dylan orders a mushroom Swiss burger, with steak fries and a club soda with grenadine and a lime wedge. As she is chatting with her group, she feels like someone is watching her. She turns her head and sees the guy from the front door quickly avert his gaze. She appreciates the look of him from afar as she tells herself she does not have time for that. She takes her career seriously and doesn't need distractions.

I listen to the conversations at my table and contribute to the conversations as appropriate. My attention, however, is on the woman across the room with her reddish-brown hair and emerald green eyes. For some reason, I just can't look away, and it appears she feels the same, as she keeps glancing over my way. Joey taps me on the shoulder.

"Hey Man, can I buy you a beer?"

"Thank you for the offer, Joey, but I am good with my sweet

tea." I say with as much sincerity in my voice as I can. I really do appreciate the offer.

He gives me a questioning look but doesn't press the issue. That wasn't so bad I think to myself. The group ordered another round of drinks, and I topped off my sweet tea. The conversation keeps flowing, as well as the drinks.

I feel like I won a personal battle as I share a little bit about myself and learn about my classmates. I have successfully avoided my past, or so I thought.

"Hey Hardy, my dad told me you used to be a paramedic with Lime County EMS. You told us you were a landscaper before applying to the academy." This came from a slightly slurred and slightly loud Lisa.

All conversation stops and everyone stares at me. This is the point where I typically bolt out of the situation. As I look around for my exit, I see emerald green eyes staring at me. When our eyes make contact, I see the face of those eyes start to smile. It instantly calms my racing heart. I take a deep breath, and I hear Sheila in my head telling me to be strong and be honest.

I take another deep breath and steady my nerves.

"Well Lisa, since you asked" I crack a strained smile. "Both are correct. I was working in landscaping when I applied, and I was a paramedic before I went into landscaping." blowing out a big breath when I finish.

"Why did you quit being a paramedic?" This came from Joey. His voice and body language showed concern for me. That made my throat tighten up. I took in a big gulp of tea.

"Well, something tragic occurred, I lost my family, and the stress became too much. I don't want to scare you from this line of work, but PTSD is real and is really hard to work through and live with. And even if it isn't full blown PTSD, many public safety workers deal with moral injury, and it has a lot of similar symptoms. It has taken me years to get to this point. I don't want to talk about it yet, but I hope to get there at some point. I love this line of work and have missed it. I worked really hard to get myself to this point." I finish quietly hoping not to see disgust in their faces.

What I saw instead was a vote of confidence and smiles around the table. "Well, if you are a paramedic, then you will be able to help us study for and pass our EMT section of the academy" Meredith says joyfully. "Also, thank you Hardy for sharing that. I can tell that it was difficult for you. When you are ready to talk about it, we are all ears. We may even learn something from your struggles that will help us."

"I've heard of PTSD but what is moral injury?" Joey asks.

"It is where events witnessed, or actions taken, or decisions made that challenge our deeply held moral beliefs and values. For instance, you are unable to rescue someone from a fire in time or extricate a person from a bad crash. One moment you're talking to them, the next moment they are dead. You did not do anything wrong, yet they still died. Another example is how we frequently witness the horrible things that people can do to each other. It challenges our moral fiber on how we feel we, as a society, should conduct ourselves. Those are just a couple examples." I say to the group.

I give Meredith a huge genuine smile. Then I smile at the group,

I can tell the mood has shifted and our group has grown even tighter. I make a mental note to thank Sheila for her confidence in me. I look over to steal another look of those mesmerizing emerald eyes and can't find them. I look around and the owner of those eyes are gone. A tendril of disappointment starts creeping up and I give myself a mental shake. I wonder what that was all about. The night continues on, and people start leaving for home. I also decided to call it a night. I pay my tab and head to my truck. I make it home, shower and crawl into bed for one of the most restful nights of sleep I have had in a very long time.

I wake up bright and early and decide to drive the four hours north into Montana to spend some time on the family land. Our family owns 20,000 acres of pristine Montana wilderness. It has been in our family for generations. To ensure it stays in our family, it has been placed in a family trust. I load up my external frame hiking backpack complete with sleeping bag, camping skillet, campfire coffee pot, ground coffee, and my fly rod. I grab a couple of potatoes, carrots and my trusty backpacking knife.

I spent the day walking around, watching all the wildlife. I also build a lean-to shelter using an already fallen tree, large branches, tree bark and leaves for insulation. I spent the late afternoon fly fishing for trout. Nothing beats a dinner of fresh trout over a fire with roasted carrots and sliced potatoes. As the sun starts to set, I gaze up and watch as the stars start to fill the sky. It is amazing how beautiful the night sky can be without the light pollution of the cities. As I start to fall asleep cocooned in my sleeping bag in my homemade shelter, I tell myself I should do this more often. I haven't been here nearly enough over the last several years. It is time I changed that. My last thought before slumber takes over is that I should build a log cabin so I can enjoy this place in the wintertime.

I wake up the next morning, and kick start the hot coals in the fire pit to brew my coffee. As my coffee is brewing, I take apart the lean-to shelter. I fully embrace the leave-no-trace camping lifestyle. Even when I am on our family land. The land was pristine when I arrived, and I want to leave it that way. I gather some water from the stream and ensure my campfire is completely out before I pack up and hike back to my truck. I fiddle around my house for the rest of the day and prepare for week three of the academy.

Monday morning I arrive at the training center for week three of the academy. The focus of week 3 was Emergency Medical Service (EMS). While we do not offer transportation to the hospital, that is provided by Lime County EMS, we do first respond to medicals in our fire apparatus. All of the firefighters in the department are certified to the Emergency Medical Technician (EMT) or Paramedic level. EMTs can provide a basic level of medical care including oxygen therapy, bleeding control, splinting, etc. Paramedics can offer more invasive care such as start IVs, administer medications, place endotracheal tubes, and use electricity to correct certain abnormal heart rhythms. While paramedics can provide more invasive care, both positions are critical to the care a patient receives. Our department is unique in that you already need to be certified as an EMT or Paramedic to apply. This allows for a shorter academy, and we need to learn the Blue River Fire Protection District way of providing care and interacting with the Lime County

EMS department.

The training cadre decided to change the order of events for week 3. PT has been moved to the afternoons. Higher temperature and more sun. I can see it in all our eyes. We all groan internally; however, no one dares groan out loud. With that announcement we settle in for more death by PowerPoint to go over our EMS charting software and policies. We learn that we use the same charting software on tablets that Lime County uses and the tablets are located on all fire apparatus. This way we can start charting and then when Lime County arrives, we are able to send the information we obtained to them. The same goes for our cardiac monitor. All the information we obtain with that, such as blood pressure, heart rate, oxygen saturation, end tidal $CO_2$, heart rhythm can be sent wirelessly to their report.

After four hours of learning about our equipment and policies, it was time for lunch. Lunch was interesting to say the least. With the knowledge that I used to be a paramedic with Lime County, my academy mates were asking me about how they operate. All of them earned their EMT certification at the local community college in preparation for this job. No one has medical transport experience. They asked very good questions about how they interact with local fire departments, is their equipment the same, and how does the stretcher operate? I could tell they were invested and wanted to learn. I also explained when I was on Lime County, it was helpful when the local fire department had the name, date of birth, and insurance card for the patient handy, as well as an initial chief complaint (what is bothering them the most, or why they called 911) as well as a baseline set of vital signs. Our lunch break flew by, and

I was glad I had something to contribute to the conversation. It felt like we were a cohesive team again.

After lunch we had another PowerPoint presentation on our National Fire Incident Reporting System (NFIRS) that we use to log all our calls. After that it was PT time. This PT rotation was different. First, we did the stair climb wearing a weighted vest. We climbed to the third level then pulled up a donut roll of 50 ft section of two and a half inch hose, then climbed to the 5th story. After that we had a 2-minute jump rope. We finished the circuit with 20 kettlebell swings then started over again. I leave the training center thoroughly exhausted and head home. I take a shower, make a deli sandwich with a few dill pickle spears, BBQ flavored kettle chips and several tall glasses of water.

Tuesday and Wednesday were pretty much the same. We have scenario-based training where we would assess and start treating the patient until transport arrives. We cover many topics such as stroke, chest pain, allergic reaction, overdose, labor and delivery, fractures, penetrating trauma, behavioral emergencies, etc. We work in teams of four. The team that is not being assessed are the role players, then we switch for the next scenario. Each day we ended with PT. I went home nervous for Thursday and Friday. On those days, Lime County was sending a paramedic unit to integrate into training with us. I hadn't been gone that long, I was sure I would recognize the paramedics in attendance.

I arrived Thursday morning and walked into the classroom. I see Beth and Trevor talking with the training cadre. My heart starts to race, and my palms get sweaty. They were two of my regular partners. I try to slip in unnoticed, but I fail miserably as I bump a table and knock several books to the ground.

"Hardy! Oh My God, it is so good to see you!" Beth cries out loudly as she runs up and gives me a hug. She was like a sister to me over the years we worked together, yet I still tense up with the contact. Sensing my discomfort, she releases me.

"Hi Beth, it is good to see you." I say with as much confidence I can muster. I really am glad to see her. The thing with PTSD and depression, isolation becomes your "friend", and you push away everyone, even those you like. Beth and Trevor would be those people. I look over and see Capt. Domingo watching our interaction intently. I still can't place where I know him. It is starting to bother me.

We go through scenario after scenario all morning working with Beth and Trevor. At first the patient handoffs were rocky, but as with everything, practice makes perfect. Everyone is feeling confident with their skills and having a good time. During a break I step outside to get some fresh air. I feel someone walk up and stand next to me. After a long pause they speak.

"Hardy, it has been a while. How are you doing man?" Trevor says quietly like he is afraid to startle me.

"I've been worse." I choke out fighting the tears forming in my eyes. Trevor and I were best friends before the fire. He tried so hard to keep reaching out to me and I kept pushing him away. Still, I find it hard to lie to him.

"I miss them so much! The pain doesn't go away." I say in a choking sob. "I am making progress, but it is hard. I'm sorry for pushing you away.  Do you still have the same number?  I still have my same number.  I tried to get rid of it, but I just couldn't."  I say as I try to gain my composure.

"My number is the same.  Will you answer if I call?  He says half joking and half serious.  "Looks like the break is over.  Are you in a good place to continue?"  Concern evident in his words.

"Yeah, I'm good.  Hey, thanks for coming to see me.  I am trying really hard to take back control of my life.  Seeing you and Beth brought back a flood of emotions.  I should have expected that."  I say with half a smile.

We walk back in, and I feel the gaze of Capt. Domingo on me as I take my seat.  I am quiet during lunch, but no one seems to notice.  Or maybe they did and just knew I needed a little space and time to gain my composure.  The afternoon PT session was especially brutal but as I finish, I realize it is because I am not only physically exhausted but also mentally exhausted.

Friday goes much the same as Thursday.  We have scenarios that are progressively complex throughout the morning.  We break for lunch, and the cadre announces there will be no PT this afternoon as they have a surprise for us.  After the initial excitement dies down, we realize we may be wishing for PT instead.  And we were right.  As we were finishing our lunch break, the training cadre came ringing a bell telling us both crews needed to respond to a motor vehicle crash involving a tour bus full of senior citizens going to a casino.  We leave the classroom building and find a literal coach bus on its side near the A building.  There are 35 people on the bus, and we need to manage the scene, triage and extricate the patients, and document their injuries and vital signs. It seems overwhelming as we hear voices in the bus. It is at this moment we realize they have live actors on the bus.

We work together stabilizing the bus, checking for hazards, and formulating a plan for evaluating how to remove the victims from the bus while triaging and providing initial treatment. Meredith and I are tasked with going into the bus. We identify 20 people who are able to move on their own and just need help getting up and over two ladders to climb out of the bus. These are identified as walking wounded and are the lowest priority for transport. With those people being assisted out of the bus by our academy mates, Meredith and I begin triaging those that can't move. We identify 3 deceased passengers based on their injuries and reported lack of life sustaining vital signs. We leave them in place for the time being. We identify 6 critical patients that Meredith and I place on backboards along with Joey who hopped in the bus to help package and remove the victims through the emergency roof openings. The last six are next to move. We bandage and splint broken extremities, and assist getting them out of the bus through the emergency roof hatches.

The training cadre gives us rare praise for our teamwork and decision-making abilities. I see legitimate smiles on their faces that last more than a second. Make no mistake, we still have two weeks left of the academy, but we all feel a sense of accomplishment. As we are cleaning up and putting everything away, it is decided that we meet at the Silver Spur again. It has become an official week ending tradition of class 20-02.

I arrived for my weekly check-in session with Sheila. I hear the familiar bell ringing as I open the door.

Sheila looks up from her computer and smiles. "Is it that time already? Wow, the week and day have just flown by. Have a seat and I'll be over shortly."

I sit down in the plush chair and get lost in thought as the past week replays in my head. I think to myself, what a rollercoaster of a week.

"You look lost in thought." Sheila says as she sits down. "What's on your mind?"

"Well, it has been an emotional roller coaster of a week. Last Friday at the Silver Spur, Lisa asked me very directly if I used to be a paramedic with Lime County. I took your advice and told the truth. Of course, the question came up as to why I no longer work there. Again, I was honest and said I went through a family tragedy that I am working through. I then said I don't want to talk about it, but I hope to get to that point sometime." I spill out with pride evident in my voice. I pause to gather my thoughts.

"That is a big step Hardy. I am proud of you. You have made a lot of progress. I can hear the pride in your voice. You should be proud". She says in a proud parent tone. "You said it was an emotional rollercoaster of a week. When a roller coaster goes up, it must come down. What else happened?" She continued with a voice full of empathy.

"Things were better with our academy cohort. The tension was lifted away. It was EMS week, and I was able to help my classmates study and learn how Lime County EMS operates as we work closely with them. Things were great until yesterday and today. Lime County EMS joined us for scenario-based training. I not only knew the paramedics they sent, but they were also my two regular partners. Trevor and Beth. Anxiety came roaring back. The worst part about it was they were so excited to see me. I treated them horribly and pushed them away, and they acted like I never did that. Trevor came up to me during a break and the floodgates opened up. I ended up apologizing for pushing them away. He forgave me just like that and asked to not be pushed away again." I finish with tears in my eyes and throat so tight I can barely swallow.

"You have good friends who care about you and want to help you." Sheila says matter of factly.

"Friends I don't deserve." I mutter quietly to myself

"Don't say that Hardy. These friends have seen you at your worst and yet are still in your life for a reason. You do deserve them. Let them in." She replies with a challenge in her voice.

I guess I muttered my comment louder than I thought.

"Hardy, no one is expecting you to forget what happened. That is impossible. What we are hoping for is for you to forgive yourself for something that happened that was out of your control. Let's make that your homework for the next week" Sheila finishes with softness in her voice. I can only nod, unable to speak through the tears and tight throat. We stand up and she gives me a reassuring hug.

I arrive at the Silver Spur and sit in my truck for a while. My mind is heavy with what has happened over the last three weeks. I have had to confront more past demons, feelings, and emotions than I was prepared for.  I feel the cab of my truck start to close in as the increase of my heart rate and breathing start their vicious cycle of sending me down that dark and lonely rabbit hole.  "NO!" I screamed out to nobody in particular.  I start square breathing and feel my body start to relax as I start to regain feeling in my hands and feet.  After a few more rounds, I feel my heart rate slow, and I return to normal breathing.

A strange feeling comes over me, and I suddenly don't want to be alone at the moment. I get out of my truck and almost run into the Silver Spur.

As I walk in, the soothing sound of the steel guitar washes over me as the cover band plays "Midnight in Montgomery" by Alan Jackson. I take a look around and spot the group at our usual table. They are talking about the crazy finish to the week and the adrenaline rush everyone felt afterwards.

""Does that happen all the time?" Lisa asks, looking directly at me

"A large-scale MCI with an overturned bus? Thankfully, no."  I replied back to her.

"No, I mean the adrenaline rush.  I was literally shaking after it was over." Lisa says with a little laugh

"It's the same rush I get with skydiving and backcountry skiing," Meredith says with a smile.

"The adrenaline rush is always there, that is a normal body reaction.  A lot of firefighters and EMS personnel will run on a treadmill or lift weights as a way to release that adrenaline. Or, like Meredith, engage in high intensity activities."  I say with a laugh while looking at

Meredith.

The waitress arrives and takes our drink order. Beer and shots of whiskey are ordered around the table. I order my sweet tea. It is then I realize I have been coming to this bar weekly for a while now, being around people drinking and I don't feel a pull to start drinking. I realize I really have made progress and give myself a mental high five.

The conversation turns from talking "shop" to what everyone is doing this weekend. Meredith is going whitewater rafting in Cody with some friends. Derrick is building a backyard playhouse for his kids. Tyler and Joey are getting together with high school friends for dirt biking and four wheeling. Dan is planning on curling up on his couch to read a couple new books he purchased. Lisa is shopping for a new vehicle. She says she is looking for a pink jeep wrangler. John is helping on his family ranch. I really hadn't planned anything but at that moment I decided I was going to call Trevor in the morning. I don't know if he is working. I guess we will find out. I tell the group I plan on reconnecting with an old friend. After a couple more rounds and good conversation, we all went our separate ways for the weekend.

The next morning, I wake up and start brewing my morning coffee. I start a load of laundry and peruse the newspaper. I am not delaying calling Trevor. I am waiting until 9am. As I read the newspaper, I see a picture of our overturned bus from yesterday. Apparently, the senior mock patients were part of a senior acting group and the article was about the group using their talents to help train the newest area firefighters by providing their services for the MCI drill. The picture shows the bus stabilized with rescue jacks, the ladders in place and someone being taken out the emergency roof hatch on a backboard. I smile as I recall the training scenario and am happy I was a part of it. I then read the part where they interviewed Capt. Everett.

*Captain, can you tell us about this scenario?*

*Yes, it is a simulated bus rollover carrying 35 senior citizens on their way to the casino. The recruits were to evaluate the scene, formulate an incident action plan based on the strategic priorities that they identify, then execute that IAP.*

*How did the recruits and actors perform?*

*The actors were wonderful. They exceeded our expectations. This is the first time we have partnered with an acting group of role players. As for our recruits, they performed as expected. They are learning and applying the knowledge learned. They have really integrated well with each other and improved their teamwork.*

It is hard to tell from a written document if it was an honest appraisal of our actions or just a puff piece for the paper. It does not make the department look good if he says the recruits under performed and have a lot of work ahead of them. I set the paper down and look at the clock. The hands on the wall clock show it is 9:05. I grab my phone, and my hands start to shake. Maybe I was in fact delaying calling Trevor. I hit the call button on his contact page before I can talk myself out of it.

"Good morning, Hardy. How are you?" Trevor answers the phone with a tone that implies we talk on the phone frequently. If he is surprised by my call, he has hidden it well.

"Are you working today?" I responded hesitantly. I'm not sure how to answer his question. How I feel is fleeting and can change on a dime.

"No, I have the weekend off.  What's on your mind?"  Trevor pushes for me to open up.

"Want to meet at Carols Corner Cafe?"  I ask for two reasons. First, I hate talking on the phone.  Second, I am hungry.  Thinking of biscuits and gravy with scrambled eggs has my stomach growling.

"Yes, I can be there in 30 minutes."  He replies

"Ok, I'll see you in 30.  Thank you."  I say and hang up the phone.

I drive over to the cafe with my mind going in a million different directions.  I know I haven't been a good friend and need to apologize. I just don't know how, where to begin, or if it will be enough.  I park and take a deep breath.  I walk into the cafe and snag a corner booth.  I order two cups of coffee and wait for Trevor.  I hope he still drinks coffee.  I study the menu as if it has the answers to all my problems.  I sense someone sitting down across from me and I look up from the menu.  I see Trevor smiling at me like he just won the lottery.

"Let's eat a good breakfast and chat for a little bit.  Then I need your help.  Eat a lot of calories.  You're going to need them."  He says as his smile grows even wider.

I stare at him for a long moment.  "What if I have plans after this?"  I replied suspiciously.  I don't but he doesn't know that.

"We both know you don't have plans.  Even after all this time you still can't lie to me with a straight face."  He says now laughing. "Besides, you owe me.  I'll consider it as part of your apology."  He finishes with a daring glare my way.

I take a big breath in.  "You're right.  I don't have plans. Whatever it is, I'll do it.  I don't deserve you to be so nice to me.  I'm sorry… for… everything." I say tears in my eyes.

"Stop with the self-deprecating BS Hardy." He says sternly. "You lived through something horrendous. I can't even imagine how I would have handled it. There is no judgement from me. The question is how can I help you heal?" His voice is full of compassion.

"Are you guys ready to order?" the waitress asks

"I'll take the lumberjack platter please with two extra eggs" says Trevor

"I'll take the biscuits and gravy with scrambled eggs, thank you" I say

"You're going to need more than that to get you through the day" Trevor says with a smirk. "You better add a side of bacon and two more eggs to his meal." Trevor says while looking at the waitress.

The waitress nods her head and walks to the kitchen.

I sat there in shock. Trevor ordered the lumberjack. That is 4 pancakes, a waffle, four strips of bacon, four sausage links, hash browns, three eggs and two pieces of sourdough toast. What did I just agree too? I wonder as I stare at him.

"So, what have you been doing these last couple of years?" He says, getting straight to the point. There is no sense in lying to him. He can read me like a book. I decided to lay out all the ugliness for him.

"Well, I was in fog until the funeral. Then I was angry at God, myself, and the world. I couldn't work for Lime County anymore. I couldn't function and deal with more tragedy. I started drinking heavily to numb the pain. I was so far into the bottom of the bottle, I wished to pass out and never wake up. I have frequent nightmares where Mary is screaming at me that it is all my fault that they are dead. I wake up in a cold sweat. One night I passed out in my front yard. My neighbor called 911. I was picked up for public intoxication. I was told I was required to attend court order therapy and 200 hours of community service. My community service was doing landscaping work around the city. My supervisor was Manny. My therapist was/is Sheila." I pause and take a breath.

Trevor stays silent while waiting for me to continue.

"As much as I hated it at first, it was my saving grace. I still meet with Sheila regularly. I worked for Manny for several years until I left for the academy several weeks ago." I finish as our food arrives. We eat in silence for a few minutes before Trevor speaks.

"Sheila is an amazing therapist. She understands the unique stressors of public safety. She has helped me stay sane and manage my emotions." He says casually, not noticing how shocking the revelation is to me. I had no idea he was seeing a therapist.

I sat there staring at him with my mouth hanging open for a few seconds until I recovered. "You see Sheila? I ask, still not believing him.

"Absolutely, I see her quarterly for a check-in. More frequently if something is starting to bother me. Dude, you are not alone. In fact, there are a lot more people checking in with therapists on a regular basis than ever. It is nothing to be ashamed of. I let you push me away because I thought you needed space. Trust me when I say this. I will not let you do it again. You are getting better, and I will be there to help you along and pick you up when you stumble. I forgive you Hardy for pushing me away. I love you like a brother, and I am glad you have made it this far.

I still stop by your house weekly and call you weekly.  Now I know why you weren't answering your door.  You were working.  I can't find an excuse for you not answering your phone or calling me back though.  Enough of this touchy-feely stuff.  Are you finished with your breakfast and ready to work out the tension?"  He asks, pushing his empty plates to the side.

"Yes, where are we going and what are we doing?"  I reply

"Follow me to my house.  I have three 70-foot trees that I fell and de-limbed.  I need help cutting and splitting it into firewood for the winter."  He says smiling like he was caught stealing a cookie from the cookie jar.

I followed him to his house.  He lives on a 50-acre plot of land 45 minutes out of the city.  He inherited the property from his dad.  The property has been in his family for 5 generations.  His house is a 2,000 square foot one level with a loft bedroom.  He is not on the electrical grid and does not have natural gas service.  He heats the house with a wood boiler.  He gets electricity from solar panels he installed 12 years ago.  He also put a well in about 10 years ago.

We get to work sawing and splitting. When he said manual labor, he wasn't kidding.  There were no chainsaws.  We had a two-person logger saw to cut one foot sections.  Then we used axes to split the wood. We worked until 8pm.  We were exhausted and only cut up a tree and a half.  Trevor came out carrying two large glasses of sweet tea with lemon.

"How does wood fired pizza sound for dinner?" he asks

"That sounds amazing" my stomach growls as I speak.  We both laugh.

We make pizza in his brick oven and finish dinner. I look over at the tree and a half still needing to be cut and split. "What's your plan for the rest? Want me to come over tomorrow?"

"I thought you would never ask. I would love the help." he says relieved. "Meet me at the cafe at 9am. We need to fuel up first."

"I'll see you there." I say getting up to head to my truck. "Trevor? Thank you for everything. And thank you for today." I clap him on the back and get in my truck. I arrive at home, shower and promptly fall asleep.

I wake up feeling refreshed. I brew a pot of coffee and pour it into a thermos. I arrive at the cafe and Trevor is already there sitting in the same booth we sat in yesterday. I sat down across from him. "Good morning." I say with a cheer in my voice that sounds foreign.

"Good morning." He replies while looking up from his paper. "Ready for round two?"

"Absolutely, I am hoping you're as sore as I am right now." I say while laughing.

"Yeah, but it feels good. Plus, it helps clear the mind." Trevor says, giving me a knowing look. "I can see that it definitely helped you get out of your self-deprecating, and self-punishing funk you were in yesterday morning." The waitress arrived and we ordered the exact same thing as yesterday.

"In all seriousness Hardy, stop punishing yourself. There are many people who are willing to help you with whatever you need. We understand why you pushed us all away, start letting us back in." Trevor says with an air of challenge in his voice.

"How can I let people back in when my heart has been shattered and splintered? I feel like it is being held together by clear tape. It wouldn't survive another round." I say with more honesty than I intended.

"I'm not talking about romantic interests, Hardy. Although don't let that pass you up when it comes along. I'm just talking about your friends. Let us help you rediscover the joys of friends and fun." He says while hiding a chuckle.

Our food arrives and we dig in consuming everything on our plates. We talk about his latest moose hunting adventure in Alaska. He decided to forgo the guided trip this time. Instead, he researched topographical maps, moose travel patterns, and Alaska Fish and Wildlife Agency reports. He hired a bush pilot to fly him to a set of coordinates in the wilderness. This is where he set up camp. He said it was an amazing adventure. He saw two moose but they were smaller than the legal limit to shoot. We talked about planning a trip out there to hunt together.

After the meal finished, we headed to his place to finish cutting and splitting firewood. We worked at a slower pace due to our sore muscles. We worked together sawing the trees into one-foot chunks. The feel and the sound of the saw was therapeutic: Zip, pause, Zip, pause, Zip, pause, Zip. The feel of the wood giving away to the blade of the saw vibrating through our hands. After both trees are cut into one-foot chunks we grab the axes and start splitting. We could go the fast and easy route and use a hydraulic splitter, but there is a certain sense of accomplishment earned from doing it yourself. We were unable to split the rest of the logs as we both reached an exhaustion level that prevented us from continuing.  We made burgers and roasted corn, cooking them over an open fire in his yard.  As I sat there eating my burger and corn, I realized I haven't felt this relaxed and content in years.  My belly and spirit full, I head home to sleep and to prepare for academy week four.

"This is your fault! You should have been there to save us! Now you are forgetting us!" a familiar voice screams through the dense fog.

"I'm sorry" I hear myself reply. My voice is so quiet I wonder if I actually replied out loud, or if it was just in my head.

"I failed you…and Wilma… and Theo."  I continue through a sobbing choke.  Tears flowing down my face faster than the rapids of the Blue River that runs through town.  My throat is wet and constricted, yet feeling as gritty and rough as the Sahara Desert.

"I will never forget you or forgive myself. I promise!"  I finish with a voice that fades away slowly into the receding fog.

I bolt upright gasping for breath as I take in my surroundings.  I see the familiar furnishings of my bedroom and I try to slow my breathing.  Deep breath in, hold, slowly let it out, hold, deep breath in and repeat the process.  After a few minutes, I wipe the sweat from my face and brush the hair out of my eyes.  "Dammit!" I yell as I realize I had another nightmare.

I look at the clock and see 4:04am.  The nightmares always wake me up at 4:04am.  That time is not lost on me as that was the time frozen in place on the analog clock in the room where they were found.  I get up, strip the bed and start the washing machine.  I then shuffle my way to the kitchen and get my go go juice going. I am definitely going to need it today.

Showered and dressed, I grab my thermos of much needed coffee and head to the training center for week four. My mind is lost in thought on the drive in as I replay the nightmare. It was different this time. She accused me of forgetting them. How could I ever forget them I think to myself. I finally felt relaxed and had fun, reconnecting with my best friend and she accuses me of forgetting them in my nightmare. That can't be a coincidence. I will need to ask Sheila about it.

"Good morning recruit class 20-02" hollers Capt. Everett

"Good morning, Sir!" replies everyone in unison.

"This week we will be learning about flow paths, ventilation limited fires, coordinating ventilation with fire attack and controlling the openings of a structure. These are critical to know, as any changes can affect the fire behavior." Capt. Everett says somberly. "We will watch several NIST videos, NIOSH videos, discuss strategies and tactics, and go through several scenarios. We will also spend time on the training ground practicing our strategies and tactics. Any questions?" Capt. Everett and Capt. Domingo seem to both hold their gaze on me for longer than they should. Do I see sadness in their eyes?

We watch several videos that talk about the danger of the chimney effect and how that relates to products of combustion (smoke, gasses, etc) move around a structure as openings are created. Fire and smoke will take the path of least resistance; we need to be mindful not to make an opening that puts us in that path with no secondary egress. Ventilation limited fires are particularly dangerous because all the elements of the fire tetrahedron (heat, fuel, oxygen, chemical chain reaction) are present except oxygen. When we create an opening (open door, window, ect) to extinguish the fire or investigate a "fire out", it can rapidly ignite and grow if you are not prepared. We quickly learn there is a lot more to strategies and tactics of firefighting than simply "put water on fire".

We need to be knowledgeable in fire dynamics, fire behavior, building construction, as well as all the fire protection features capabilities and limitations. All of these need to be considered while shaping the incident action plan and strategic priorities. While developing an IAP and strategic priorities is the responsibility of the incident commander, firefighters must understand all components and how their tasks support the successful completion of the strategic priorities and overall IAP. It is a lot to take in.

"Oh man, there is more to this than I realized. The more we learn highlights what little we actually know." Joey says to me during a break.

"I agree. I feel like I know just enough to be dangerous." I reply with a laugh.

After the break we gear up and go out to the class A building. The training cadre (with help from Engine 2) starts a fire with wood pallets and straw. Windows and doors are systematically opened, and we are able to see how that changes the thermal layering and movement of smoke. In one scenario, a bedroom window on the second floor was opened. We could see the smoke slowly start to make its way up the stairs. Once the window behind the fire was opened a flow path was created and the speed and intensity of the smoke increased. A few more scenarios allowed us to see firsthand what we learned in the classroom and how our actions affect fire behavior and the products of combustion.

The rest of the week went by in a blur as we spent the majority of our time in the training buildings or PT sessions. It was long and exhausting, but fun. We completed many training scenarios using offensive strategies, defensive strategies, transitional attacks, and VEIS. The last one is an acronym for Vent, Enter, Isolate, Search. It is a rescue technique most frequently used when there are defensive fire conditions in a building but it has a tenable space that can be isolated from the rest of the building, such as a bedroom or other smaller space. It is typically conducted by opening a window, climbing in, closing the interior door and searching the room and leaving the way you came. It is used if someone on the outside either knows or thinks someone is in that room.

We all gained confidence in our abilities to improve our skills. We were running like a well-oiled machine. We faced challenges head on and used our critical thinking skills to adapt and overcome the different scenarios put in front of us. We were 80 percent complete with the academy and had our final week before we joined our new shifts and stations. There was no guarantee we would work with each other. We will be placed in the open spots.

Friday after our PT session, the instructors had us meet in the classroom to discuss the final week. Monday and Tuesday were days to work on skills we felt we needed the most improvement on. Wednesday is Mock day. That day we will stay at the training center for 24 hours to simulate a shift. We will be responsible for day-to-day chores (cleaning the station, apparatus checks, training session, PT, as well as responding to mock calls. We will staff two apparatus, an engine and a ladder. We needed to elect two to operate as apparatus captains. Meredith and I were elected. I was elected as engine captain, Meredith was elected to ladder captain. We would then have Thursday off. Friday was an admin day. We were preparing our uniform for the graduation ceremony taking place on Saturday afternoon. We were also filling out other paperwork and learning our assignments for our probationary year. The final week was going to fly by.

I walked in to meet with Sheila at 6pm. The bell chimes as the door opens and Sheila looks up. "Congrats on completing week 4 Hardy" she sings through the big smile on her face.

"Thanks, one more week and I am done and onto my station assignment." I reply through a big grin.

"How was your week" Sheila sits down in the chair across from me

"It was interesting. I reached out to Trevor. We pretty much spent the weekend together as I helped him cut and split firewood. He acted like I never pushed him away. He also told me he meets with you on a regular basis. That surprised me. He has his life so put together; to hear him say he meets with a therapist was a gut check." I say timidly like a child afraid of being chastised

"I meet with many individuals for a variety of reasons and needs. Many are in a good place and want to meet to keep it that way. "

"I just never thought it would be someone I knew. The weekend was good. We had a good conversation. He called me out for my behavior towards him and my other friends, yet welcomed me with open arms, if you will.  It felt good to open up to someone else about my struggles. Then Sunday night I had another one."  I say as I close my eyes.

"Another nightmare? Tell me about it."

"It was the same yet different because this time she was also accusing me of forgetting about them. It was as if she knew I was feeling happy for the first time"

"Hardy, it appears you are having a crisis with your conscience. You may have been feeling happy but I think deep down you still won't allow yourself to be happy.  There is still work to be done with allowing yourself to be happy."

"How can I allow myself to be happy when they are dead because of me?"  I retorted back.

"That is your homework for next week.  Reach out to Trevor, put yourself in situations to be happy.  What happened was tragic, I know you blame yourself.  You and I have read the same reports.  It was an act of nature that resulted in deaths.  You are not to blame.  You have to believe that. You will have a very hard time moving forward until you do"

"Thank you, Sheila.  I know what the reports say, but if I hadn't kept the propane grill next to the kitchen sliding glass door, it never would have happened. You have never given me bad advice.  I will work on trying to be happy."

I leave and drive to the Silver Spur to meet up with my academy mates.  As I drive, "Cowboy Songs" by George Birge is playing on the radio.  I sing along to the catchy song and my mood lifts.

I walk into the bar with the cover band playing "Mountain Music" by Alabama. Couples are dancing and the tables are full. I spot our group at our usual table and as I walk towards them it feels like someone is watching me. I look around and don't see anyone looking at me. I sit down at the table and exchange hellos with everyone.

"So, my dad says Monday and Tuesday are a test." Lisa says out of the blue.

"Why does he say that?" This comes from Meredith

"The training cadre wants to see if we work together to help each other improve or if we isolate and focus on ourselves. Basically, are we ready to work as a team." Lisa replies back to the group.

"Good thing we already decided to work as a group on PT and more training evolutions!" exclaimed Joey. "I guess we already passed that test."

Everyone clinks their glasses together in a "cheers" to that statement. As I lean back and look around the bar, I see emerald green eyes focused on me from the other side of the bar. As soon as our eyes meet, I shiver, and the eyes look away. Those eyes, I have never seen a more vibrant green than that. I mentally shake my head. I can appreciate beauty from a distance but, nothing more, that only leads to indescribable pain.

"What about you Hardy?" I hear John ask as my focus returns to the group.

"What about me?" I asked, embarrassed I did not hear the topic being discussed.

"Where do you hope to be assigned after graduation? pipes up

Joey.

"I'm just happy to be back in this field, I'll go wherever." I say honestly

"I heard Capt. Domingo is a hard ass and no one but his current FAO likes to work for him.  He has two openings because no one sticks around. My dad says he is a cranky old timer who needs to retire.  No one is ever good enough for him.  People put in their year assigned to him and bid off as soon as they can." Lisa says

"So, which two of our group are the lucky or unlucky souls stuck with him?" Dan contributes to the discussion. Well, that explains all the looks he has been giving me I think to myself.  He probably thinks I am too old to be starting out.  But that doesn't explain why he looks so familiar to me. Joey and Tyler hope to work the same shift and preferably on the same apparatus, although both admit the same apparatus is a long shot.

Losing interest in the conversation, I look back over to find the woman with the emerald green eyes and to my disappointment, she is gone.  Get a grip of yourself Hardy, I say mentally.  Nothing good will come of that so stop searching.

We all leave the bar for our last weekend as recruits.  Next weekend we will be probationary firefighters for the Blue River Fire Protection District.  I give myself a mental fist pump.

I wake up Saturday morning to the bright sunshine filtering through my window right onto my face.  I hear the familiar call of the pheasants in the area as I stare through the dirty window to the trees in the back.  I should really clean those windows today. Mind made up, I get out of bed and saunter down the hallway to start the coffee. With liquid pick me up in the works, I shower and dress in jeans and a flannel long sleeve shirt. With my mug of coffee in hand, I make my way outside to work on my newly created chore list. On tap for today is to clean out the gutters and wash all the exterior windows and window screens. The cottonwood trees have gone to seed, and it is making a mess of everything.

I spend the morning cleaning out all the debris from the gutters. I make a mental note to do this every year and not wait five years between cleanings. The monotonous task allows my mind to wander. For once, my mind doesn't wander to memories of them. I think about how far I've climbed out of the hole of pain and despair. While my resolve stands not to let anyone get too close, I am beginning to realize I can start living my life again. I break for lunch and make an egg salad sandwich with a couple of pickle spears, kettle chips and an iced tea.

That afternoon, with the radio blaring my favorite 90s country hits, I continued with washing my windows and window screens. The window screens take longer than I anticipated due to all the cottonwood seeds stuck in them.

"Good afternoon, Hardy!" The voice pulls me from my thoughts. I turn and see Mrs. Miller, my next-door neighbor staring at me.

"Good afternoon Mrs. Miller. Did you need help with something?" I say slightly concerned. I moved to this house a couple of years ago and I can count on one hand how many times we have spoken. I am pretty sure she is the one who called me in when I was passed out in my yard, but I don't know for sure.

"No, nothing of the sort. Forgive me if I'm being forward. I was watching you today and felt compelled to come speak with you. You seem different… um in a good way. It was clear you were dealing with something when you moved in. I have noticed a change in the last few weeks, and I just want to say whatever has brought on the change, or whatever you have been doing, keep at it, I am proud of you." She says in a motherly tone and gives me a hug.

"Uh…thank you Mrs. Miller. I don't know what else to say." I respond in total shock at both her forwardness and total honesty. As she returns to her house, I return to my window screens shaking my head. I think to myself… Old people, the neighborhood busybodies since the beginning of time. I laugh out loud at that thought.

I spend the rest of the afternoon with the windows, window screen and weeding the flower garden that I have neglected. I should plant new flowers here and I decided tomorrow I will go shop for some flowers to plant. As I am cleaning up my tools, the realization hits me. In the stages of grief, I have hit acceptance. I know the stages are fluid and I may slide back at times, but I have never felt acceptance of the situation I have found myself in. Words cannot describe how it is to feel acceptance for the first time.

I decided on grilled salmon, cilantro lime rice, and roasted Brussel sprouts for dinner. After dinner, I start a fire in the fireplace, settle into my comfortable lounge chair and settle in to read. I found the whole series of books written by Ian Flemming at the library. In my opinion, they are so much better than the movies of these books. The books have so much more detail.  Growing sleepy, I crawl into bed and promptly fall asleep.

The next morning, I make my way to the flower nursery and pick out marigolds, snapdragons,  a couple of sunflowers, and some dill. With my haul loaded up, I head back home to plant.  I spent the morning planting my flowers.  That task finished, I admire my work and head inside.  I walk inside and hear my phone ringing.  I answer without looking at who it is.

"This is Hardy."

"Hey Hardy, it's Trevor.  Are you doing anything this afternoon?"

"Just finished planting flowers and trying to decide what to do next."

"Want to meet at Jackies Sports bar?  The Rockies play at 3pm."

"Yeah, that sounds great.  It has been a while since I watched the Rockies play.  I'll see you there."

I pull into Jackies at 2:45 and see Trevor's Bronco in the lot.  I walk in and find him sitting at a high top with a perfect view of the big screen with the pregame show on.  I sit down next to him as I clap him on the back.

"Thanks for the call and invite."

"Thanks for actually answering and coming."  He retorts with a laugh.

"Ouch… I guess I deserved that. Touche."

The waitress arrives.  Trevor orders a club soda with lime. I ordered an iced tea with lemon.  We also get the chicken nacho platter with jalapenos of course, fried mushrooms, and fried pickles.  The game starts and they are taking on the Twins.  We watch the game in silence for a while as it turns into a pitchers duel.  The third inning ends with a score of 0-0 and only one hit for each team.

"So, Mrs. Miller called me yesterday afternoon."  I choke on my iced tea as the words come out of Trevor's mouth.

"How do you know Mrs. Miller and why would she call you?" I say, thinking this is a very weird conversation.

"Well, she is the neighborhood busybody and she saw me stopping by your house frequently to check up on you. One day she came out to confront me.  We talked for a while and I explained I was a close friend and you were going through some things.  I gave her my number and told her to call me if she noticed something different with you."

"I want to be mad at you for that…but I just can't be.  Why did she call you?"

"She told me you seemed very different in a good way and she wanted to report the good news."  He says smiling.  "What happened that she would call me to say that?"

"Well, I was outside yesterday cleaning my gutters, windows, and window screens with the radio on."

"And this morning you were planting flowers. Something is different with you."

"I think I have finally accepted what happened. I'm still grieving and I miss them terribly.  But I have resolved to move forward with my life.  These last few years have been miserable. I want to start living my life again."

"It's good to have you back, my friend." He says unable to hide the smile growing on his face.

We watch the rest of the game in content silence. The Rockies end up winning in the bottom of the ninth inning with a single shot home run. It was a pitchers duel the entire game. The Rockies win 1-0 with two hits for the Rockies and one hit for the Twins. I drove home still full from our feast. I curl up with my book and read until I am tired. Tomorrow is the final week of the academy. I feel like a small child on Christmas Eve night.

Monday morning, we all arrived and decided to complete our PT session first thing. We had a lot of pent-up energy that we needed to dissipate. With a good workout to calm our nerves, we chose to spend the rest of the morning working on sets and reps with hose line management, ground ladder deployment, and forcible entry. During our lunch break, we asked the cadre for a couple of vehicles for tomorrow so we can practice auto extrication. The cadre said it was a great idea, and they would contact the salvage yard and have two vehicles delivered for tomorrow. That afternoon we spent the time practicing our search techniques using fake smoke to limit visibility in the class B building. The class B building is set up like a 2 story single family home with an attached garage. We also practiced our mayday drills, down firefighter rescue, and self-rescue. All in all, we felt confident with our skills and being operationally ready for our probationary status.

Tuesday morning, we again started the day with PT. The excitement was palpable, and we needed the exercise to calm our nerves. We then moved on to auto extrication and perfected our techniques using the cutters and spreaders, rams, stabilizing jacks, and airbags. We practiced single door removals, whole side removals, roof removals, dash rolls, etc. By the time we were finished with the vehicles, they looked like Lego building sets with pieces of the vehicle stacked back on the frame. After lunch, we practiced our medical assessments and treatments of patients. We practiced cardiac, stroke, allergic reaction, altered mental status, trauma, obstetrics related, and pediatric scenarios. We also reviewed our medical guidelines. We felt as prepared as ever for our final test, mock shift day.

"Recruit class 20-02!" Hollars Capt. Everett. Everyone stands at attention. "Shift change is at 0800 hours. Dismissed." He finishes, never one to speak more words than necessary.

I wake up at 5am and am too excited to sleep any longer. The last time I remember being this happy was my wedding day. I immediately shut down that thought. I do not need to spiral down the depression hole. Feeling like I just dumped a bucket of ice water on myself, I get dressed to go for a run. I decided to run my favorite 10-mile loop. I need to burn off this nervousness. As the miles go by, I run by the Structural Designs Architectural Group building. I can't help but look at the building, as it is so unique. As I am running by, I see emerald green eyes looking out a second story window. It takes my brain a second to catch up. I stop and turn back around, searching the windows. No one is there. I shake my head thinking I have lost my mind. I continue my run and turn back towards home.

Dylan is in the office early. There was a problem with the latest design. If she doesn't fix the problem by the end of the week, they will lose the project. The only problem is, she doesn't understand what the customer doesn't like. She asked for clarification but only received a vague response. She had heard rumors that this customer was difficult to deal with. Was that the plan all along… set her up as the fall guy? she thinks to herself. There is so much male ego in this field. Maybe that is why the customer doesn't like it, because it was designed by a woman. She knows she is intelligent and has earned her place to be here, her thoughts continued.

"AHHGGG." she yells out as she grabs both sides of her head. "I will get this project to the clients' liking. Challenge accepted." she resolves as she stands up to walk to the window. The view of the city always calms her nerves. She looks out and sees a quiet city on the verge of waking up. Well, quiet except for one person running down the sidewalk. Maybe that's what she should do, she thinks to herself. Mind made up, she will go for a run to clear her head. She turns around to grab her workout bag. She heads to the restroom to change and go for a run.

Back home and showered, I grab my travel mug of coffee and head to the training center. I have Joey, Tyler, and John on the engine with me. The others are with Meredith on the ladder. At 0745 hours I ensured we all had our correct gear and we placed it on the engine. I designated John as the FAO. He was responsible for checking the engine and all exterior cabinets to ensure we had everything we needed. I had Joey checking all our medical equipment. Tyler was checking all the gear in the cab of the engine and performing SCBA checks.

I had to meet with Meredith and our "Battalion Chief" for the day, Capt. Domingo. He gave us the schedule for the day and also laid out his expectations. He expects the apparatus to be clean, the station to be clean, and for everyone to participate in PT. He also expects apparatus turnout times to be under one minute during the day and under two minutes overnight. We have a school group of second graders for a fire safety talk at 10am. The ladder will handle that. There was also a presentation at noon on falls prevention for a group of senior residents of an independent living apartment building. The engine will handle that.

I leave the meeting and help the crew wash the engine. We decide on a menu for dinner and take up a collection to purchase the needed supplies. Because we are not allowed to drive the apparatus on the city streets. the BC goes to the store to get the supplies. We decided to start on station chores. I grab the broom to start sweeping. BEEP

BEEP BEEP… Engine 1 responded to 1234 Main street allergic reaction.

We jump into our places on the engine and start heading to the class B building. 45 seconds.  I give myself a mental high five.  We park and I grab the tablet, Joey grabs the cardiac monitor, Tyler grabs our first in bag and John grabs the airway bag.

Lisa meets us at the door playing the role of the daughter.  We walk in the house and find Meredith sitting in a chair playing the role of the patient.  We questioned the patient and family, determined it was a bee sting, and obtained vital signs. verbalize we would start an IV and start one on the practice mannequin. We then drew up epinephrine 1:1000 and Benadryl.  We then administered the epi intramuscular (IM) and administered the Benadryl via IV.  We obtained more vital signs and performed patient hand off to the verbalized arrival of Lime County EMS.

Clearing the call, we returned back to the station and began our station chores.  Station chores include sweeping/mopping/vacuuming the floors, cleaning the bathrooms, cleaning the kitchen, washing the windows, etc.  While we are cleaning, a school bus full of children pulls up and the ladder crew goes to greet them and present the fire safety lesson.

The engine company goes to the A building to sweep out and wash down the hallways, rooms, and stairwells from the residual straw left over from live fire burns.

BEEP, BEEP, BEEP… Engine 1, Ladder 1 respond to 1236 Main Street for a fire alarm sounding.  Called in by an alarm monitoring service. We gear up and get in the engine. We head over to the storage barn and announce our arrival. BC 1 is already on scene and directs us to go inside and investigate.

Leading the crew, we make our way inside and glance at the fire alarm annunciator in the main entryway. It says attic water flow. We continue our search for smoke, fire, or water flowing from a sprinkler as Ladder 1 arrives. BC 1 directs them to ladder the roof, investigate, and provide a roof report.

We did not find any smoke, fire, or water flowing inside. The ladder company found nothing unusual with the roof. BC 1 advised us to make our way to the alarm panel and attempt to reset the alarm panel. We reset the alarm, and it was holding in normal operations. We all clear the scene just as a bus of seniors arrive for their falls prevention presentation. We greet the seniors as the ladder company goes to the B building to sweep and clean out the rooms and stairs.

After the falls prevention presentation, we eat lunch. After lunch we sit around the kitchen table chatting and discussing various topics. We go on a few more medicals, while the ladder goes on a lift assist, and elevator rescue.

We fit in a group PT session as well as put out a dumpster fire. We work together to make dinner and after the meal is finished, we clean the kitchen. When the chores are done and garbage is emptied, we sit down and relax in the lounge room. Someone turns on the TV to the Rockies game. They are in Arizona playing the Diamondbacks. At 9pm everyone heads off to their bunks.

BEEP BEEP BEEP. Engine 1, Ladder 1, BC 1 responded to

1234 main street dwelling fire. Everyone jumps out of their bunks and rushes to the apparatus. We are geared up and rolling in one minute and 55 seconds. Phew, that was close to the two-minute standard. BC 1 arrives and establishes main street command. He performs a 360-exterior evaluation off the building and advises there is a working fire on the first floor charlie/ delta corner of the house. Engine 1 is tasked with pulling a cross lay and performing a primary search and fire control of the first floor. Ladder 1 is tasked with securing utilities and performing a primary search of the second floor.

John engages the pump of the engine while Joey deploys the line and sets up for an interior attack. Tyler grabs the irons and checks the front door. It is locked. Tyler forces entry and controls the door with his Halligan. Joey signals to John that he is ready for water. The line charges and Joey checks and opens the nozzle so John can set the correct pressure. Line ready, we are masked up and make our way inside. There is moderate smoke banking about halfway down the floor. We start a right-hand search to make our way to the charlie, delta corner. Joey is leading and advancing the nozzle, Tyler is pulling the hose line for him while searching and I am scanning the area with the thermal imaging camera.

We didn't find any victims on our way to the seat of the fire. We find the fire and extinguish the flames we can see. I radio to command that we have fire control and that we are continuing our primary search and checking for hot spots. Ladder 1 reports that primary search off the second floor is complete. Ladder 1 is reassigned to set up a fan at the front door for ventilation. We finish our primary search of the first floor and radio that we have an all clear. Command clears all companies, and we return to the station. Both crews respond to a couple more medicals overnight.

We wake up at 6:30 and brew a pot of coffee. We sit around the table talking about the shift and shift life waiting for shift change to occur. The clock strikes 8am and Capt. Everrett dismisses us. We all leave for home and have a much-needed morning nap.

"So, what do you think of the recruits?" Capt. Everett says while eyeing Capt. Domingo over his coffee cup.

"I think they are going to do well here. I would never tell them that to their face though. I don't want them to relax and get too comfortable. They are probies and need to earn their place." Capt. Domingo says as he downs his cup and gets up to refill.

"And what do you think of Morrison? He is older than a typical recruit. and he has that haunted look in his eyes already. Do you think he will last long?" Everett says as the shoulders of Domingo stiffen.

"I'll be honest just this once and because it is you asking. Seeing him brings back bad memories. I'll never forget that day. He is resilient, in fact I want him and that young cocky son of a gun Whitman on my crew."

"You never want probies, are you ok?" Everett asks, coffee cup halfway to his mouth in utter shock.

"Yeah, I am.  I don't believe in coincidences.  The good Lord put us both in this academy for a reason and I am going to listen to Him and take a hint.  As for Whitman, I'll wipe that cocky grin off his face and whip him into shape."  Domingo says with a faraway look as he thinks about his wife and the life they had built. They always wanted children, but it was never in His plan.  Maybe, just maybe, he and Morrison can help each other. "I'm going to head out.  See you tomorrow, Everett." he finishes as he picks up his phone, dials a number and hits the call button.

Hi! You've reached Rosalie…. You know what to do after the beep.  BEEP.

"Hey sweetheart, it's me.  I just wanted to hear your voice.  I can't believe it has been 5 years since you were taken from me.  I miss you so much.  Well… until we meet again."  Domingo hangs up the phone, a single tear falling from his eye.   "I always thought I would be the one dying of cancer, not her.  It isn't fair." he says out loud in the car to no one in particular.  Well, maybe he meant for Him to hear it.

I wake up after what I thought was a short nap only to realize it is two in the afternoon.  I decided to go for an afternoon hike in the mountains.  It is such a nice day, it would be a waste to spend it indoors. I grab my hiking backpack that has emergency supplies, just in case I need it. I park at the trailhead and grab my pack. It is seventy degrees with white puffy clouds in the sky and a slight breeze. It is a perfect day for a hike. I like this trail head as they have a two mile, a five mile, and a ten mile option. I chose the 5 mile option and anticipate it will take me two to three hours to complete. I send a text to Trevor that I am hiking the 5 mile option at the trailhead and anticipate being back around 6pm. It is always a good idea when heading out into the wilderness alone to notify someone of your plans and anticipated return time. It just may save your life if something happens.

I enjoyed my hike and saw plenty of wildlife along the way. It was a great way to decompress and rec-center myself. I make it back to the trailhead at 5:45pm and send Trevor a text that I am back. I received a thumbs up as a reply. He must be working, I think to myself. I drive back home for a shower and dinner. After dinner, I decide to watch a movie and pick Spaceballs. It is a hilarious comedy that has me laughing out loud. Feeling tired, I crawl into bed ready for the final day of the academy.

I wake up Friday morning to the birds chirping, the turkeys gobbling, and the sun shining. I hop out of bed, make my way to the kitchen and start the coffee pot. I then jump in the shower and get dressed. Finally, I make my bed, grab my coffee and head to the training center.

I arrive with my academy mates, and there is excitement in the air. We spend the morning ironing our shirts and pants, polishing our name plates, badges that will be pinned tomorrow, as well as polishing our shoes. Everything is inspected by the cadre and no surprise, everyone has something to "fix". I get the feeling it did not matter how well everything was done, something would need to be done better. We break for lunch and decide to go to a nearby cafe. I ordered a half salad, half sandwich and iced tea for my meal. It was delicious and we had good conversation guessing where everyone would be placed.

After lunch we filled out our benefits enrollment forms with HR and learned our shift, station, and apparatus assignments. Meredith was assigned to B shift Engine 5, Lisa was assigned B shift Engine 1, Derrick was assigned A shift Engine 3, John was assigned B shift Engine 3, and Dan was assigned C shift Engine 4. Tyler and Joey were split up much to their disappointment. Tyler was assigned A shift Engine 1. Joey and I were both assigned B shift Engine 2 with Capt. Domingo. I look at Joey and his face is pale. He is thinking the same thing I am: What did we do to piss off the training cadre to have been placed with the reported crusty curmudgeon?

The last thing we had to do before leaving was pick someone special to us to pin our badge. For everyone else, that was easy. It was a spouse, boyfriend, girlfriend, parent, or grandparent. For me, I have no one, I have a sister that is 20 years older than me, we don't talk, and my parents were older when they had me. They have passed away. I literally have no one, I think. Then I send a message to the one person that could be an option. He sends a message back and says he wouldn't miss it for the world and would be honored. That settled, I head home. My standing meeting with Sheila is cancelled due to a family emergency.

Graduation is in the auditorium of the performing arts center in the downtown section of Blue River. We all look sharp in our dress uniforms. We peek out and see the auditorium full of soon to be coworkers, friends, family and community members. I see Trevor chatting with a few firefighters.

The Chief of the department approaches the podium and asks everyone to stand. Once everyone is quiet, the color guard proceeds to post the colors. We are signaled to start our march to our seats on the stage with the pipes and drums playing.

Once seated the chief talks about the fire service in general and traditions we hold, then gets specific to the Blue River Fire Protection District. He highlighted the accomplishments during the academy and thanked the training cadre for their tireless effort. Lastly, he thanked us for our dedication during the academy, for joining this noble profession, and well wishes for a successful career with the BRFPD.

One by one, we are called up to shake hands with the administrative staff and training cadre. Then our chosen person pins our badge, and we pose for a picture. I watch as my academy mates make the rounds and return to their seats.

"Hardy Morrison", I hear the chief announce. I stand and walk, shaking hands. Trevor is at the end with a big smile on his face. I get to Trevor and he pins my badge then gives me a big brotherly hug. I am slightly tense. I am not a fan of close physical contact. Trevor knows that and makes it quick. I stifle a chuckle as the line 'brothers don't shake hands, brothers gotta hug' goes through my head as I remember the line from some movie I watched. I know that is exactly what he is thinking too. I make my way to my seat. We finish the ceremony with our oath of position.

With the ceremony concluded we all agree to meet up at the Silver Spur for one last group get together. A shift has to report to work Sunday, C Shift on Monday, and B shift on Tuesday. I invite Trevor to join us and head home to change out of my dress uniform. The BRFPD has a very strict policy against wearing a uniform in an establishment serving alcohol, even if you aren't consuming. It is an image and perception issue.

I arrive and the place is packed. I had to park on the street about a half a block down. I walk in and do not see our group. The hostess sees me and says we are in the back party room. I walk to the room and find about 50 people already there, including Trevor. I can start to feel a panic attack coming on. So many people in such a small room. I almost turn around and leave but Trevor sees me and instantly knows I am ready to bolt. He approaches me as he says "Take a deep breath Hardy." I do and start to feel a little better. I take a moment to center myself and then we head into the room.

Meredith sees me first and runs up and slugs me in the shoulder. "Congrats old man, you survived the academy" she says while laughing. "There are apps, and drinks, including several pitchers of iced tea for you." she says over her shoulder as she moves on to greet others arriving.

I grab an iced tea and make my rounds as well. I start to relax and join in on several conversations. I find out during conversations that Meredith reserved the room a week ago knowing full well we would all end up here. I give her some money to help cover the cost of the apps and drinks. Trevor finds me and says he is heading out. He has a 6am shift.

"Congrats, don't be a stranger and stay safe." he says and turns to leave.

The party is winding down and there are not many people left.  I stay and help clean up and put the room back in working order.  Once everything is cleaned up we all promise to stay in touch and meet up when we can.  We all can't meet up as we are on all three shifts, but we resolve to get as many of us together as we can, when we can.

I head home and sit down on my couch letting out a deep breath. What a busy and exhausting day.  It was fun, I am drained but still unable to sleep.  I turn on the TV and find a professional bowling tournament broadcasting.  Perfect, this will help me fall asleep.

I wake up the next morning still on the couch.  I was clearly tired. Normally, I would wake up in the night and move to the bed.  I fiddle around the house all day completing minor tasks on my to-do list.  My mind, however, is on my first shift day tomorrow with Capt. Curmudgeon aka Capt. Domingo.  I guess I'll find out why no one sticks around on his crew.  I remind myself that I am probationary, so I must suck it up, put in my time, keep my mouth shut and bid out when I have the chance.

I eat dinner and head to bed early.  My first shift starts at 8am.  I better arrive at 07:30 to not be on his bad side on day one.

3

I wake up to my alarm at 5am.  I have a lot of nervous energy
and did not sleep well last night.  I decide to go for a short 5 mile run.  I
put my earbuds in and take off.  The music soothing my racing mind.  As
I keep going, my muscles loosen up and my thoughts clear.  Today is my
first day and I resolve to make the most of it.  Returning home, I start
my coffee and jump in the shower.  Dried and dressed, I turn on the
news while I make my breakfast of yogurt with honey and a banana.  I
read the newspaper while I eat and see a picture of the academy
graduation and see all of us sitting on the stage with the chief speaking.
I finish breakfast, wash my dishes, and grab a thermos of coffee.  I make
sure everything is tidy as I won't be back until tomorrow morning.

I drive to station 2, it takes about 20 minutes.  It is in an older
part of town that needs some revitalization. The median income of the

residents is on the lower end and the properties are in various stages of neglect. I arrive at station 2 and give it a double look. It definitely fits the neighborhood motif. This station looks to be about 60 years old. It has two apparatus bay doors that are closed. Ladder 2 and Engine 2 are housed here. It was one of the original stations from the volunteer firefighter days. I step out of my car and see Whitman arriving. He has the same look on his face that I imagine is on mine. Utter shock and disbelief.

We walk up to the building and noticed the entire side is water stained and dirty. We open the door, walk in and are immediately assaulted by a musty dampness smell. We look around the apparatus bay and don't see anyone. We place our gear by the engine and walk to the lounge to find everyone else. The chatter of the off-going crew sitting around the table comes to a screeching halt as they notice us standing there.

"You must be Domingos' new chew toys." someone I couldn't identify said out loud causing the entire table to roar with laughter.

"Probationary firefighters Morrison and Whitman reporting sir" I say to the unidentified person.

"Don't call me sir, I work for my paycheck. No need for formalities with me. Little pro tip… Don't let Domingo see you in the lounge in the morning. Your truck should be checked and ready to go before your shift starts." Whitman and I scurry back out to the apparatus bay and hear another round of laughter behind us.

We are checking the medical equipment on the engine and trying to memorize what is in each bag and where the bag is located when we hear "Morrison, Whitman, my office now". We put the bags back and step out of the engine. Capt. Domingo is turning away from us and walking down a hallway. We hurry to catch up.

We round the corner into the captain's office and notice the water stains on the wall and carpet. We stand at attention waiting for him to speak. He eyes us for a good long minute, his bushy horseshoe mustache making him look like he has a perpetual frown.

"Welcome to C shift Engine 2. The station may not be pretty but that's ok, we are the busiest engine and won't be spending much time here. I am going to explain my expectations. You do as you're told when you're told. I don't tolerate freelancing. On the fire ground or other emergency scene you do exactly as I say. As far as station chores are concerned, they will be completed immediately after you check the equipment on the apparatus. I expect all chores to be completed as soon as possible. The equipment check should be the first thing you complete as we typically have a call right out of the gate. Next, we will train"...BEEP BEEP BEEP Engine 2 breathing problem 478 4th ave SE.

We look at Capt. Domingo waiting to be dismissed as he barks

"What are you waiting for, you heard the voice in the ceiling.… GET MOVING!"

We turn and hurry to the engine climbing in the back and putting our seatbelts on. After what feels like forever waiting, we see Capt. Domingo and who we assume is our FAO approaching the engine laughing.

"False alarm boys, the off going shift thought they would have a little fun." says the new person.

"Ok, Whippe enough Tom Foolery. Time to get back to work." Capt. Domingo says roughly as he starts walking back to his office. We follow him knowing our lecture was not complete.

"As I was saying, we will train every afternoon. I don't tolerate mediocrity. You will know every aspect of your job and perform as expected. There is always room for improvement, and I expect you to get better every day. I want you to look through your workbooks and identify what area or skill you would like to train every shift. I expect that decision to be made by 9am so we can pull the lesson plan and prepare for training. Lastly, this is most important. You will treat our residents with respect. What may seem like fun to you could quite possibly be their worst nightmare and we need to act accordingly." Capt. Domingo finishes while staring directly at me as if we were sharing some bond.

For a moment, I think I see kindness and understanding in his eyes. Then just as fast as it showed… it was gone.

"Yes sir" Whitman and I say in unison.

"Dismissed." says Capt. Domingo turning his attention to his paperwork. I look at Whitman and we both look at the clock …8:05. I look at him again and he nods.

"Capt. Domingo, for the training today, we would like to work on SCBA donning, doffing, and troubleshooting." I speak. Capt. Domingo nods his head but does not verbally reply. Taking the hint, we leave his office and head back to the engine to finish our equipment check.

We work on the station chores doing our best to clean a station that clearly needs a remodel and upgrades. Whitman says he will tackle the bathroom and locker room. I will tackle the kitchen and lounge. We will clean the hallways and bunk room together. While cleaning, we meet the other 5 people out of our station that staff Ladder 2. They seem nice as we say hellos. I notice they keep their distance from Capt. Domingo and Whippe. I don't sense tension per se, it is more of a you do your job and I'll do mine type of vibe.

BEEP BEEP BEEP… Engine 2 respond Whispering Pines Senior Living 3685 Stillman Ave for a possible stroke. Whitman and I rush to the engine, jump in the back and place our seatbelts on. We see the other two moving quickly to the engine and jump in. Ok not a prank I think to myself.

Whippe drives the engine out of the bay and the lights and sirens turn on. He drives fast and efficiently, yet safely. We arrive ahead of Lime County EMS and I grab our first in bag and cardiac monitor. Whitman grabs the oxygen bag.

We are directed to the second-floor room 210. I am the first one in the room and see an elderly female sitting in her lounge chair with the right side of her face drooping slightly down. Her eyes meet mine and I can see a hint of panic in them.

"Ma'am, my name is Hardy. We are here to help you. What is your name?" I say, wanting to assess her speech as she tries to respond.

"Mm..Mir…Miri." She stops frustration evident.

"That's ok. Just try to relax while we continue our assessment and get you ready for transport to the hospital. I say as reassuringly as I can. There is a staff member present. While Whitman obtains vital signs,

I turn to the staff member.

"Her name is Miriam Johnson.  She is 79 years old."  The staff member says.

I get other relevant demographic information to pass along to the transport crew.

"When was she last seen normal" I ask

"I helped her wake up and get dressed, and down to breakfast. That was at 8:30. I helped her sit in her chair after and came to check on her at 11am and found her this way." She replies

"Blood pressure 190/110.  Heart rate 70.  Oxygen sats 96% room air.  Blood glucose 110. Arm drift right side as well as weak grasp." Whitman announces.

Yep, sure seems like a stroke and it was noticed early.  That is good news for Miriam.  We update Lime County via the radio and I start an 18 gauge IV in her left AC.

Lime County arrives and we complete our hand off and help load Miriam into the ambulance. We get back in the engine, clear the call and return to the station.  We restock our EMS gear and continue with our chores.

After a quick lunch, we complete our SCBA training under the intensive supervision of Capt. Domingo and Whippe.  Even though we feel we have completed the drill to a satisfactory level, they continue having us complete sets and reps.  I get it, it helps build muscle memory. Even if I feel like a small child being chastised, they really are trying to help us get better.  I don't take it personally.

We respond to a few more calls for service that afternoon; a fire alarm, a couple medicals and a portajohn toilet on fire in the park.

All nine of us sit around the table for dinner. There is good conversation around the dinner table. The awkwardness between the ladder crew and engine crew from earlier seems to have dissipated.

BEEP BEEP BEEP ladder 2 respond 1684 11th Ave SW elevator rescue. The ladder crew jumps up from the table and heads to the ladder. Dinner was finished so Whitman and I start clearing the table and cleaning the pots, pans, and dishes. Whippe helps us by drying dishes, which catches us by surprise. Typically, this is a task that is completed by the newest members.

With the kitchen cleaned, Whippe lounges in a recliner and turns the TV on to a hunting show. Whitman and I grab our tasks books and look at what we want to train. We review all the JPRs in our task books and debate several before deciding on one.

Tired from our long day, we head to the bunk room and find our cots. Yep, this station doesn't have dorm rooms like some of the other newer stations. It has two bunk rooms. We lay down on our cots and promptly fall asleep.

It was a restless night as we were up 4 times. We responded to two medicals, a fire alarm, and a vehicle fire. We thought it was a busy shift but were informed that it was a slower than average day. We work again on Wednesday and then have five days off. This department has a non-traditional 3-week rotation. Week one, we work Tuesday and Friday. Week two, we work Sunday, Thursday, and Saturday. Week 3, we work Monday and Wednesday. I think I am going to like it because every third weekend is a five-day weekend of no work. 8am rolls around and the oncoming crew is ready to go.  We all go our separate ways.  I am looking forward to a morning nap.

After my nap I wash and fold laundry and clean the house up.  I decide I am going to the family land for the extended weekend so I want the house picked up and cleaned.  I reach out to Sheila and scheduled a meeting for 10am Thursday since we cancelled our Friday meeting.

The Wednesday shift is a lot like Monday.  Whitman and I get settled into a routine for our station duties.  I notice that Whippe is very detail oriented with ensuring the engine is ready to respond.  He checks everything on the outside compartments, operates every tool and even checks tire pressures and fluid levels to ensure the engine is operational.

Our afternoon training session is similar to Monday.  Capt. Domingo is very demanding.  He has us go over the topic again, and again, and again.  As frustrating as it can be, I appreciate that he wants us to know the JPRs inside and out and be able to perform flawlessly.  It is clear he has high expectations for us.  Our knowledge, skills, and abilities need to be top notch or he is not satisfied with our progress.

The call volume increased and we responded to 13 calls in 24 hours.  It really is a busy station with a captain that pushes you to be better.  It is exhausting and fun, but I am ready for my extended weekend in the woods.

I leave the station at 08:30 and decide to stop at a cafe for breakfast before I meet with Sheila.  I order my breakfast and sip my coffee and stare out the window at the people walking by on the sidewalk.  I notice a woman power walking down the street wearing a beige pencil skirt and blue blouse.  She is average height and has an air of confidence with her.  I can't help but watch as she walks down the sidewalk. I'm not a creepy peeping tom, I just feel drawn in.  As I am watching, her face turns in my direction and we make eye contact. Bright emerald green eyes hold my gaze as electricity starts running through my body.  It is those emerald green eyes that I have seen several times now over the last few weeks.  The exact same.

After what seems like minutes, although probably only a few seconds, she breaks eye contact and shakes her arms and head.  Who is she and did she feel it as well, I think to myself.   My breakfast arrives and I dig in.  I finish my breakfast, leave cash on the table for a tip, grab my bill and head to the cashier stand to settle the bill.

"Hello Hardy.  How are you today?" Sheila says as I walk through the door.

"I'm feeling tired but good. How is the family?

"We are good.  Grandma gave us quite a scare, but she is getting better. So, the academy is finished and now what?"

"Yep, we graduated and I have been assigned to C shift engine 2. The captain is interesting.  He has a reputation as an old crusty curmudgeon.  He expects a lot out of us and requires a lot of training. He is also very closed off.  He is unapproachable."

"Who is your captain?"

"Capt. Domingo."

"Ahh ok.  Are you sure he is the one closed off, or maybe are you still keeping walls up and keeping people out? Think about that and evaluate how you are contributing to that."

"Yeah, maybe I am."

"So how do you like the job now that you are out of the academy?"

"I love the job, it is great to be back out helping people, and the fire side of the job is fun as well. It is a different dynamic than working strictly EMS. The 24-hour shifts can be long, but now I have a 5-day weekend and did not have to take any vacation."

"I'm glad to hear you are enjoying it. Do you want to continue weekly check-ins or what do you want/need?"

"I think we could go monthly at this point and readjust if needed."

"That is a good plan. Let's get you scheduled."

I arrive back home and do a quick check of the house to double-check that windows and doors are closed and locked. I grab my back country gear that I used for extended trips, my fly rod, dried nuts and fruit, root vegetables and load my truck. I double check that I have what I need. I hit the road excited for the next few days camped out under the stars.

I arrive at the edge of the land and turn on the access road. I drive about a mile down and park the truck. I grab my gear and start hiking. The sun is shining, and it is 65 degrees out. I stir up a few deer while I walk. I am heading towards a grove of trees that are near the small river that flows through the land. It is my water and food source.

The grove of trees provides good shelter. I have decided to build a small one-room cabin with a loft and wood burning stove. This weekend I am scouting a good area to build. I want it near the river on a flat part of land. This will give me a good project to work on to occupy my time and thoughts. I build my temporary lean-to shelter, and fire pit before I go and catch my dinner.  Already feeling the tension leaving my body, I sigh in peaceful content.

"Great job on closing that project.  That is a difficult customer to deal with.  I knew you could do it!" Dylan looks up and sees her boss standing in her office doorway.  She had finally resolved the issues with the client and won the design contract for the group.

"Thank you, that means a lot.  It was touch and go there for a while.  Difficult is an understatement. I can finally catch my breath and wrap my head around it." Dylan responds with a smile.

"I mean it.  You put in a lot of hours over the last couple of weeks to close it out.  I really appreciate the effort and dedication.  I know it is only Wednesday morning but take the rest of the week off to take some time for yourself.  The way I see it, you already worked your hours for the week, and I have no other projects for you."

"Thanks, I will see you on Monday then." Dylan replies as she finishes up on her computer and shuts it down. Things are lining up, she thinks to herself.  Her mom had called just that morning asking when she was coming home because she hadn't visited in a while and as much as her dad will deny it, he could use an extra set of hands with the ranch. She calls her mom as she leaves the office.

"Hey mom, change of plans, I have been given the rest of the week off for closing a deal. I'm coming home. I should be there by dinner." she says unable to hide the smile in her face.

"That is great honey, your father and I are thrilled to see you again. Drive safe. We love you"

"I will. I love you guys too." She says as she hangs the phone up.

Her smile grows even bigger as she thinks about spending the next few days on the ranch with her horses away from the bustle of the city. She arrives home and quickly changes clothes and packs her bags. She hits the road and says Montana here I come.

She arrives at her family ranch around 4pm. She steps out of the car and deeply inhales the clean country air. She grabs her bag and heads towards the steps of her childhood home. It is a two-story farmhouse with a porch that wraps around the entire home. It is still painted in faded blue with white shutters. She walks in the house and finds her mom in the kitchen pulling a roast out of the oven and placing an apple pie in next.

"That smells amazing!" she says to her mother as she walks in.

"Dylan! Come give your mother a hug." Her mom says as she comes around the center island, apron covered in flour. "I'm so happy you're here. It gets lonely at times with your father running the ranch and all you kids leaving the nest." Tears start to form in her mother's eyes.

"Mom, you're going to make me cry. I wish I could come back more, but my career is taking off and I am doing what I set out to do."

"I know honey, and I am proud of you. We both are. It just gets lonely at times with you kids gone making your own mark on the world." she sniffles. "Dinner is almost ready, why don't you go grab your father. He will be thrilled to see you. I think he is in the barn." she says as she guides me to the door.

Dylan walks out of the house and passes the horse corral. Her horse, Daisy, trots up to the fence. She is a beautiful dark chestnut colored morgan horse.

"Hey Daisy, how have you been?" she coos to her horse. Daisy nuzzles up next to her as Dylan strokes her head. "We are going to go on some rides while I am home. Sound good to you?" Daisy neighs in response. "Ok, good. I'm going to go find dad for dinner. I think we will go for an evening sunset ride tonight."

Dylan opens the barn door and sees her dad in the middle of re-shoeing a quarter horse.

"I'll be in for dinner shortly dear." He says not looking over his shoulder.

Dylan doesn't want to spook the horse or her dad so she stays quiet until he has finished with the hoof he is working on.

"Hey dad, I just got in and mom sent me to tell you dinner is ready." Dylan says with a smile on her face.

"Hey Dilly Bear! Come give your dad a hug!" He replies using her nickname as he turns around.

She wraps her arms around him soaking up his warm comfort.

"It's good to see you kid." as he kisses the top of her head. "I've got one more hoof to finish and I'll be in."

"Want some help?" she asks hopeful

"This one is content and easy, but I could use the company if you don't mind. With just your mom and I here it gets lonely at times."

"So how is the ranch doing?" she says changing the subject. She is starting to feel guilty for following her dream.

"The ranch is good. I have a couple more ranch hands as I am getting too old to do everything. How is work in the big city?" He says changing the subject from the ranch.

"It is going really well. I just closed a huge deal for our group. I love designing buildings and bringing the customers' ideas and visions to life." she says as her smile grows wide. "I wish I had more time to come back here more often. I miss the wide-open spaces and you, Mom, and Daisy of course."

"We miss you too. Let's head in and clean up for dinner." He says as he finishes, picking up his workspace.

Dinner was full of questions about Blue River and her job. While she loved her job, she really missed being out here. Her mind was strolling down memory lane bringing with it a feeling of nostalgia.

"Are you dating anyone?" the question from her mom bringing her mind back to the dinner table.

"No. I am focusing on my career. I don't have the time or energy to date anyone." she replies with a curt tone in her voice.

She is tired of the pressure to date, marry and have kids. That may be how her mom feels where Dylan should be at this point in her life, but that life does not interest her.

"I know you get tired of hearing it, but honey you need to find a good man to settle down with." her mom says exasperated.

"Mom, I don't want to argue. I know how much you enjoy the domesticated life and that fits you, that isn't who I am. Plus, I haven't found anyone that I share a connection with. I am perfectly content with the life I have." she says, trying to keep the peace.

"I know you are honey, it's just that life around here is lonely and your father and I were hoping to have some grandbabies that we can dote over." Her mother says quietly.

And there is the real reason for this conversation Dylan thinks to herself. Her thoughts continue as she thinks even if she did get married, she doesn't know if she would even want kids.

"Thank you for dinner. I think I am going to take Daisy for an evening ride." She gets up and clears her dishes.

"Hey Daisy! Ready for a ride?" Dylan asks as she approaches with her saddle. Daisy neighs her affirmation.

With her saddle secured, Dylan climbs up and they start off down a trail towards the river edge at a slow trot. Daisy and Dylan meander along the riverbank for a while as the sun slowly fades in the sky, allowing her mind to wander. She thinks about the guy she saw in the cafe earlier that morning. There was something familiar about him as if she knew him from somewhere. She starts to get goosebumps and shiver like she did this morning. It is getting chilly out, might as well head back in before it gets too dark.

Dylan makes it back to the barn and sees the silhouette of her dad leaning up against the barn. She slowly leads Daisy into the barn and into her stall for the night. Dylan dismounts then removes the saddle.

As she is brushing Daisy, she can feel the stare of her dad. She ignores it for as long as she can. She is still quite mad about the marriage and baby lecture from her mother. Thankfully her dad breaks before she does.

"Ya know, mom doesn't mean anything by it. It is just the way she was raised. She loves you; you do know that right?" he says rather hesitantly. Which is unusual for him. He is genuinely straightforward and to the point.

"Of course I know she loves me. It's just there are times I don't think she knows me." Dylan snaps a little too forcefully and cringes a little bit. "Look, maybe it's because you and mom have set an impossible standard for what a relationship looks like. I have yet to find anyone that I see myself having the type of relationship you guys have." Dylan sighs with the truth finally out.

She puts her parents' relationship on a pedestal of perfection that no one can measure up too.

"Is that what you think? Our relationship is perfect? Well on one hand I'm glad we were able to successfully hide all the bickering from you." He laughs out loud at his little joke. "But now I'm questioning if we did the right thing because we have painted an unrealistic picture of what marriage looks like." He ponders to himself.

" Dilly Bear, there are things that I do that annoy your mother, and there are also things that she does that annoy me. That is part of any relationship. My advice, if you're willing to take it, is to open your eyes and heart to the one who does the small things for others. The one who is selfless, but not a doormat. The one who does the small little things to help others without even a second thought. Even trivial things that just seem second nature to do. Those are the type of people that outshine the imperfections they have. Everyone has imperfections, even you, your mother, and I." He finishes with a tear in his eye.

Dylan's eyes are misty as well.

"Dad, you always know what to say to me to get me out of my mood." Dylan says, giving him a hug.

"Well, between your mother and yourself, I have had a lot of practice." He laughs out loud.

I head into work reflecting on the last 6 months. Whitman and I have made huge progress in improving our skills and teamwork. We have a close bond, and I view Whitman as the younger brother I never had. I don't know what to make of Capt. Domingo though. The guy is so hot and cold. One shift I feel like the captain approves of my skills and the next shift, he is yelling at me about all the mistakes I am making. I shake my head as I pull into the station parking lot. I look at the deteriorating station and heard a rumor that the department is exploring how to fund a new station.

I throw my bag on my cot and meet Whitman at the engine. We check our EMS gear and then SCBAs and other equipment in the cab of the engine. With our morning checks done we head to the lounge for a cup of coffee before we start the daily chores.

BEEP BEEP BEEP Engine 1, Engine 2, Engine 3, Ladder 2, Ladder 3 Battalion 1 Dwelling fire 64291 175th St.  Whitman and I jump up and rush to the engine.  We gear up and get in putting our seatbelts on.  The engine heads out of the bay and towards the address.

"Looks like we are going to be first in." Capt. Domingo yells back from the front. "Black smoke in the sky," he adds.

Whippe parks the Engine just past the house to leave room for the ladder on the alpha bravo corner.  Whitman and I are stepping out of the engine to deploy the hose line when we hear "Rescue Delta side second floor window, rescue Delta side second floor window." We realize Capt. Domingo is yelling at us.  We switch gears to grab our ground ladder, hook and irons as Capt. Domingo gives a size up on the radio.

"Dispatch, Engine 2"

"Engine 2"

"Engine 2 is on scene 64291 175th, 2 story single family home small in size with a working fire.  Engine 2 is performing rescue of residents hanging out of the second-floor window delta side.  Engine 2 has 175th command." Capt. Domingo says with a calm and even voice. Whitman and I place the ground ladder and Whitman climbs the ladder. He comes back down carrying a small child that looks lifeless and hands her to me.  He looks back up and the mother is no longer in sight.  I notice the child is unconscious, however, her chest is rising so I know she is breathing.  I hand her to a police officer while I climb the ladder to assist Whitman.  Capt. Domingo is completing a 360 around the house looking for other victims.

I see Whitman at the top of the ladder, and he carefully sweeps the floor with his hook. He looks back at me "She is laying on the floor. I'm going to lift her up and hand her out to you." I acknowledge and start climbing as he carefully climbs through the window.

"Dispatch 175th command" I hear over the radio.

"175th command" dispatch replies

"360 complete. No additional victims found. Walkout basement. Kitchen fire charlie side.  Offensive strategy. One rescued so far working on a second rescue." He updates sounding cool as ice on the radio.

"175th command, Engine 3 approaching." Capt. of Engine 3 announces.

"Engine 3 Pull cross lay off Engine 2. Primary search fire control first floor through side alpha."

"Engine 3 copies.  Line off Engine 2. Primary search fire control 1st floor through Alpha"

Whitman lifts the woman up onto the window ledge and into my arms cradled like a baby.  I hear "I have your spot" from the bottom of the ladder as Capt. Doinngo returns to us.  I climb down with the woman draped across my arms. I can't tell if she is breathing.  I step onto the ground and carry her towards the street curb.  As Whitman climbs out, I lay the woman down on the ground.  I do a quick visual assessment and see her chest rising up and down.  Whitman arrives at my side with the monitor and oxygen bag.  We obtain vital signs and administer oxygen when Lime County EMS units arrive.  They take over patient care and transport both patients to the hospital.

I take a deep breath and realize for the first time that all the other apparatus have arrived as well as BC 1. BC 1 assumed command from Capt. Domingo as we recycle our air bottles as we are assigned primary search of the basement. Engine 3 has fire control of the kitchen fire. We make our way into the basement. There is moderate smoke but no fire. We conduct a right handed search and search every room. We do not find any extension or other victims.

As we pack up our engine to return to the station, Capt. Domingo approaches us. He looks pissed. "What took you so long to make the rescue!? We taught you better in the academy! That slow pace is unacceptable! We will be doing more ladder drills. That will not happen again!" spit flying from his mouth as he gives us a butt chewing. Whitman and I look at each other with confusion. We weren't slow. Captain Domnigo walks off to meet with BC1.

"We were not slow." Whitman says to me

"No, we had rescued one victim and were working on victim two when he made it back around. I don't know who pissed in his cereal this morning." I respond back to Whitman.

My own anger rises as the weight of the situation hits me hard. This is exactly how they died, because rescue wasn't there in time. Sure, you can save these two, but you couldn't save them, could you? The voice in my head mocks me in a condescending tone.

"Hey, he doesn't mean that. He is just stressed." Whippe says as he approaches us. "You guys did a fantastic job. I heard they are both going to survive because of you." He finishes while clapping us on the back.

"Stressed or not, it doesn't give him the right to take it out on us." I say to Whippe.

Pot meets kettle. That voice in my head pokes at me. Like you should be criticizing him.

We arrive back at the station and I am fuming mad. I shower, change into a new uniform. I then proceed to the captain's office.

"Sir, I respectfully disagree with your opinion that we were slow on the rescue. We had made one rescue and were working on the second rescue when you came around the side. Is there room for improvement? Sure, there always is. But the fact is, those two are alive because of the actions we took. We didn't sandbag or lollygag. We moved with purpose safely and performed two rescues. I am open to criticism but not a butt chewing when it isn't warranted." I spill out before I lose my nerve.

He stares at me for a long moment. It is unnerving. Is he going to discipline me I think to myself.

"Is that so?" he says while still eyeing me up.

"Yes, Sir." I say with more conviction that I feel. He continues to stare at me, not blinking.

"Dismissed. Get back to work." he responds and turns back to his computer.

I go back out to the apparatus bay and walk laps. I am so angry. I start washing the fire truck for something to do to release this tension. Whippe saunters up to me.

"You have cajónes, I'll give you that. No one ever challenges the captain. Especially a probie." He chuckles.

"I'm not some greenhorn twenty-year-old with no life

experience.  I know his kind and at times they need to be called out, no matter the rank.  Respectfully of course."

"Don't judge him too harshly.  You don't know him or his history.  That isn't his first rescue like that.  In fact, he has been on calls where victim rescues aren't possible.  Like I said, he was stressed. If I know him like I think I do, don't worry, the most punishment you're going to get is extra station duties for challenging him.  I have been his FAO for a very long time.  Avoid him and let him think it through.  You guys did a great job, but don't let it go to your head.  We can always get better, especially probies." He turns around and walks away.

The rest of the shift seems to crawl on by.  Whippe was right.  I was given extra station duties.  I had to wax not only the engine but also the ladder truck.  I'm sure I will have other 'duties as assigned' tasks for the next few shifts.  In between waxing the fire apparatus, we went on 7 medical calls and 3 fire alarms.

I also received a call from Trevor right before the end of shift. He heard about the rescue and was calling to congratulate me and asked if I wanted to talk about it. I tell him I don't want to talk about it right now.  He pushes back and tells me he knows me too well.  He knows my mind is at war with itself.

"Hardy, if you won't talk about it with me.  Please see Sheila. You need to talk through this. You have made such great progress. Keep that progress going."

"I'll think about it." I say

"Ok, call me anytime if you need to talk.  Gotta run, we are getting a call."

I hang up the phone and walk out to my truck. I am exhausted and plan on sleeping before making any decision about talking to Sheila about this.

"This is your fault! You should have been there to save us!" a familiar voice screams through the dense fog.

"I'm sorry" I hear myself reply. My voice is so quiet I wonder if I actually replied out loud, or if it was just in my head.

"I failed you…and Wilma… and Theo." I continue through a sobbing choke. Tears flowing down my face faster than the rapids of the blue river that runs through town. My throat is wet and constricted, yet feeling as gritty and rough as the Sahara Desert.

"You could save them but you couldn't save us. Did you not love us enough?" The shrill voice reverberates through the fog

"I will never forgive myself. I promise! I love all of you more than you know." I finish with a voice that fades away slowly into the receding fog. I fall forward on my knees and I keep falling over a cliff.

My eyes jolt open as I hit something hard. I look around and realize I am on the floor next to my bed. Sweat dripping down my face, I am panting trying to suck in as much air as I can. I look at the clock. It is only 10am. I was asleep for only an hour. I change my bedding, shower, and lay back down in bed. I am too tired both physically and emotionally to do anything else.

Unable to fall back asleep, the rescue plays over and over in my head.  Only in this twisted version, there are three victims: Mary, Wilma, and Theo. They are crying out for me and I can't reach them.  Tears start to roll down my cheek as I look at the picture of them on my nightstand. They must have been so scared, and I wasn't there to save them.  I saw the terror on the woman's eyes before she passed out.  I imagine that was the look on Mary as she tried to comfort the kids telling them everything will be alright.

I must have cried myself to sleep as I wake up to pounding on the front door.  "Go away." I say meekly, too tired to move.  the pounding stops only for my cell phone to ring.  Not even looking at whose calling I silence the phone and roll over.

"Get out of bed Hardy.  I'm putting an end to this pity party." The voice of Trevor startles me as my eyes shoot open.

"How did you get in here?" I ask in shock.

"A fake rock with a hidden key?  Really, you couldn't be anymore stereotypical Hardy." he laughs as he starts turning lights on.  "Get up and get dressed.  You and I are going fishing.  I heard about the rescue. I also know that had to hit you hard.  By the looks of it, I am right.  I said I wasn't letting you push your friends away again.  This is me sticking to my word.  Get up and get dressed."  He turns around and leaves the room.

I have known Trevor for a long time.  I might as well get up because he is not going to leave. I look at the clock, it's 2pm.   He should still be at work I think as I get out of bed and into the shower.

I make my way down the hall to the kitchen following the scent of coffee.

"Aren't you supposed to be at work?" I ask as he hands me a cup of coffee.

"Yep I am." He replies matter of factly with no explanation.

"So why are you here?" I ask already knowing the answer.

"Because when somebody didn't answer their phone after repeated attempts, I asked Mrs. Miller to come over and check on you. She came over, saw your truck in the driveway and knocked a bunch of times but you didn't answer. She called me back and said something doesn't feel right. So, I took PTO for the rest of my shift and here I am." He says as he stares at me daring me to tell him he is wrong. We stare at each other for a long moment in silence. "That's what I thought." He continues breaking the silence. "Get your fishing gear and get in my truck. We are going to fish and talk this out."

I relax on the boat rocking in the waves as the current moves us down the Blue River. The sun is beating down with a slight breeze. I almost feel relaxed but that is a false sense of security as I wait for the interrogation session to begin. But it doesn't come. After an hour and a half, I break the silence.

"Thank you, Trevor." I say out loud.

"Your welcome Hardy." He doesn't ask what for. He knows.

"That was a crappy situation you found yourself in. You did a hell of a job holding it together while it was unfolding. That speaks volumes to how far you have come in the healing process."

"When I left work, I felt fine, I thought I WAS fine. I took a nap and woke up on the floor by my bed. I had another nightmare. Then I couldn't fall asleep and was looking at the picture of them, thinking about what they endured and putting their faces on the victims that we rescued. I couldn't stop myself."

"No offence Hardy, but I could tell from our conversation this morning that you were not fine. It's why I tried to check in with you so many times and sent Mrs. Miller over to check on you."

After four hours of fishing, while dragging a line up and down the river, we didn't catch any fish. Still the impromptu therapy session worked. Trevor dropped me off at home and I made dinner and curled up in my chair to read for a while.

I arrive for our next shift and complete all our morning duties when Capt. Domingo and the ladder captain gather everyone around for an information session. We all look at each other wondering if it is an impromptu training or public education event. "I wonder if they are retiring and riding off into the sunset." Whitman whispers next to me.

"I doubt it. We couldn't be that lucky." I whisper back.

We listen to them ramble on about the state of the fire station and the safety risks it poses. How some testing came back and shows high levels of mold, mildew as well as some structural integrity questions. Because of that we are going to be housed and stationed out of the public works building just down the road. We are informed it will be tight quarters, but we are going to have to make due as they build the new station. Everyone's ears perked up at that.

"Are you serious?" someone from the back pipes up

"Yeah, if this is a joke, it isn't funny." Another ladder guy says.

"They have been saying we are getting a new station for the last 5 years. I'll believe it when it happens."

"Well, you can believe it starting right now." the Chief of the department says as he comes around the corner. "We are in negotiations with an architectural design group to design the new station. We value input and we find it only reasonable, considering all of you will be working out of it, to give you a voice in its design.

Now, obviously we have a budget to consider but any reasonable idea or suggestion will be considered, as long as we stay within budget. We will have a representative from the design firm meet with each and every one of you to go over what you would like to see included. I don't have an exact time yet as we are still in negotiations with them, but I can reasonably assume it will be within the next month."

4

Dylan logs into her computer to check her email. As her systems are logging in, she looks out her window and sees the bustle of the downtown landscape. After spending over a week back home on the ranch, the bustle of the city seems to have lost some of its allure. After speaking with her dad the first night, it was clear he needed help. So, like the ever-faithful daughter, she took the next week off of work. She didn't have any current projects, and she was close to maxing out of her vacation hour accrual. Lastly, who knew when she would have the chance to take a week off again.

Shaking herself out of her daydream, she starts weeding through her email. She sees an urgent email from her boss asking to meet about a proposed contract with the City of Blue River. She is intrigued by the idea of working with the city.  She wonders what they want to do.  She emails her boss and says she would love the opportunity.  She spends the next few hours going through her 785 emails that she accrued during her week and half vacation.  This is why you don't take vacations, the voice inside her head says.  As she is designing some buildings just for fun, seeing as she currently doesn't have a project to work on, her boss sends her an email. It says meet in conference room one at 1pm to meet with the city about the proposal.  She looks at her watch and it is 11:30am. She decides to take a walk and go out for lunch.

Walking down the street in the bright sunlight has reenergized her. As if on auto pilot, she walks to her favorite cafe.  She sits down in her normal booth and the waitress approaches.

"You want your usual Dylan?" The waitress asks

"Yes please" Dylan replies.  Maybe I come here too often if I sit in the same booth and the waitress knows my order.  She shakes her head to clear that thought. As she waits for her food, she stares out the window watching everyone walk by wondering what their stories are.

"Here you are dear.  A mushroom swiss patty melt, steak fries, and a sweet tea. Need anything else?" the waitress asks as she looks at Dylan.

"No. This looks amazing. As always. Thank you." Dylan replies as she digs in.

With lunch finished and her tummy full she sets down enough cash on the table to cover her bill and leave enough for a generous tip. This waitress has been here for a while, and she knows the waitress is paying her way through college without taking student loans.  Dylan considers this a pay it forward type of situation.

Back in the office, Dylan grabs her tablet and heads off to conference room one to meet with the city about their proposal. Trying to make a good impression, she sets out fresh carafes of ice water, coffee, and hot water with an assortment of different style bags of tea. While she is genuinely a coffee drinker, to each their own is what she has always been taught.

The city representatives have arrived and as she suspected the city manager is in attendance as well as the building official. To her surprise, the fire chief and fire marshal are also present. Ok, it must have something to do with the fire department she thinks to herself. This will be interesting. She has never worked with the city government before, let alone a fire department. Lastly, her boss arrives at the predicted 15-minute late mark. He has to make it seem like he is a busy person even though he has all of us to complete the heavy lifting. Perception is everything she thinks to herself.

"Ok, everyone is here. Let's get this meeting started." Her boss says "Marty, would you like to start?"

"Yes, of course. I have brought along the building official as they will be signing off on all building permits, as well as the fire marshal, as they will be signing off on all fire code permits, and the fire chief, as the building in question will be to replace an aging fire station." The city manager starts. Very cool she thinks, she has never designed a fire station before. What a challenge!

"We are looking to replace a fire station that was built in the 1960s. It is well past its replacement timeline, beyond its growth potential, and quite frankly not cost effective to refurbish and add on. We would like to tear down and rebuild in the same location." The fire chief says.

"So, what are you looking for in respect to design? More traditional fire station look, More modern? I can pull up some pictures of fire stations that have been designed across the country if you would like?" Dylan speaks up

"Here's the thing, we would like to give our firefighters a chance to give their input on the design and features of the building. After all, they are the ones who will be living and responding to calls from there." The chief replies "We would like you to meet with each firefighter and each shift to gather ideas and tally the ones that are mentioned most often. We have nine firefighters on each shift and three shifts so that would be 27 firefighters. Would you be able to do that?" The chief finishes

"I can meet with them. That is not a problem. Do you want them to come here, or should I meet them at the fire station?" Dylan asks in return.

"Well, here's the thing. The fire station has been condemned so would it be possible for you to meet them at the public works building? That is their temporary station until this project is complete." He says rather sheepishly. Wow, she thinks to herself. Condemned? Yep, this project is long overdue.

"Yes, I could meet them there" Dylan looks at her boss for confirmation and he just nods his approval.

"Great, the vote goes to the City Council on Monday next week to approve the design contract.  We would like to get started as soon as the contract is approved." The chief asks, clearly nervous about the short time frame.

"Absolutely, and I will gather photos of stations that have been built recently, both traditional and modern, in the event anyone needs help picturing ideas." Dylan says to the group.

"Ok, now onto the cost.  We have a budget that we cannot overrun as we are accountable to the tax levy.  I have asked around about others that have contracted with you, and I believe we are in a similar price range." The city manager speaks up.

"I assure you we can come to an agreement on the price for the design. I assume you have others giving you proposals given that it is tax money being spent?" Dylan's boss speaks up.

"Yes, we are required to obtain three requests for proposals or RFPs to ensure we are getting a good deal for services rendered." The city manager says. "The other two have already submitted their proposal. Can you have your proposal submitted by the end of the week?"

"I assure you we will be competitive with the others. We will have our proposal submitted by the end of the week." Her boss finishes.

With the meeting ending, they exchange business cards and the fire chief gives Dylan the address to the public works building.  Dylan blocks off her calendar and leaves conference room one heading to her office to start her research on fire station designs.  Excited with the new opportunity to expand her portfolio, she dives right in.

I arrive at the public works garage to start my shift. While not ideal, this is a better building than the fire station. I resolved to make the best of the situation. A meeting room was turned into a bunk room, and the kitchenette was turned into a makeshift kitchen with electric skillets to compliment the microwave. A large grill was also placed outside. There is no oven but most meals can be made on the electric skillets and grill. Again, not ideal but we can make it work.

I find Joey at the engine checking all of our gear and supplies. I go and join him, and we finish checking all our medical equipment and SCBAs. With that finished we move on to washing the apparatus and feeling generous, we also wash the ladder.

"This place is so much better than the station." Whitman says with a smile on his face. "I don't smell the mildew and mold."

"We don't have much of a kitchen, but we'll make it work. There was only one bunk room in the station so that isn't any different." I reply

"I heard that the architectural design company hired is going to meet with all of us to get ideas for the new station. How cool is that!" Joey continues with a smile on his face.

"Really? I didn't hear that. If that is true, it will be awesome. Where did you hear that?" I ask him.

"I've gone on a date with Beth, an admin assistant, and she told me that is what is being discussed." He says his smile is growing wider.

"I hope it is true but don't believe everything you hear. Firehouse gossip can rival any high school in the county." I say with a laugh. We head over to the other conference room, that is our makeshift lounge, to start cleaning.

BEEP, BEEP, BEEP come across our portable radios.  Engine two respond 7865 Pinecrest road.  34 Year old female labor pains.  Joey and I make an about face and head to the engine.  As usual, Whippe navigates the engine quickly and efficiently.  We arrive before the ambulance. I grab our first in bag, along with an OB kit, just in case there is an imminent delivery.  Whitman grabs the oxygen bag and monitor.

We walk up to the front door and a man meets us at the front door. "Thanks for coming.  I tried to get her in the car, but we think the baby is coming."  The man says.

"Ok, I'm Hardy.  This is Joey.  Where is she?" I ask

"She is in bed.  Her water broke and she has increased cramping" He responds rather calmly.  That is not the typical reaction we see.

"How far along is she and what number baby is this?" I ask

"She is 41 weeks along, and this is our fourth child." He replies.  Ok, that explains why he is so calm, I think to myself.  This is not their first go round.

"OK, what is your name and what is her name?"  I ask

"My name is Jim and her name is Naomi."

"Hi Naomi.  My name is Hardy and this is Joey.  We are with Blue River Fire.  We are going to help take care of you until EMS arrives. Are you currently having contractions?

"Not right now" she says

"Ok, let me know when your next round of contractions start so I can time them. When did your contractions start?

"About 30 minutes ago. Ow, Ow, Ow, contractions are starting." She says through gritted teeth. I glance at my watch to start timing.

"OK, let me know when this round ends." I say as I start opening the OB kit. Joey is obtaining vital signs.

"Any complications expected with this pregnancy?"

"No, and the contractions have stopped." she says. I look at my watch and they lasted one and a half minutes.

"Ok, let me know when they start again. Are you allergic to any medications?"

"No."

"Do you have any medical history? Diabetes, breathing problems, heart problems, etc?"

"No, I am healthy and don't take any medicine besides my prenatal vitamins."

"Ok"

"Another contraction is starting" She says through gritted teeth. I look at my watch, only 90 seconds between contractions. Oh boy, or girl, we are delivering the baby right here I think to myself.

"Ok, Naomi, with how quickly the contractions are coming and that this is not your first child, we are going to prepare to assist you in delivery here. I am going to examine you and see if you are crowning. Ok?"

"Ok, I think I feel like the head is close." she says

I examine her and I can see that she is bulging. I don't see the head yet, but we are close. "Jim, she is very close. I need you to go to her and help coach her with her breathing." I say to him.

Jim nods and grabs her hand. "Joey, I need the chucks pad and some blankets. Then set up the bulb suction, clamps, and scissors.: I say as I put the sterile gloves on over my nitrile gloves.

"The contraction stopped." Naomi says.

"Ok, this next time we are going to push with the contraction. We are all set up and ready. My guess is it will be in the next minute or so."

"Hey Hardy, what do you have?" I hear Trevor say behind me.

"Hey Trevor, Imminent delivery, 4th child. Contractions are about a minute and a half in length 90 seconds apart. Not crowning as of last check but she feels pressure. No complications expected." I reply to him.

"Sounds good, everyone keep with the assigned plan. We will deliver here, then transport to the hospital." He announces to the group, confirming the plan.

"Another contraction is starting!" Naomi yells

"OK push push push push." I say as I watch and see the head start to crown. "I see crowning, you're doing really well Naomi."

" AHHHGGGG!" Naomi yells as she pushes again. I put slight pressure against the baby's head as it comes out to prevent the baby from coming out too fast. I quickly check to ensure the umbilical cord is not wrapped around the neck.

"Push again, let's get the shoulders out, then you are done pushing." I put slight pressure down to allow the left shoulder to come out, then I put slight pressure up to allow the right shoulder to come out.

I carefully wrap the baby in a towel and grab the bulb suction and suction out the mouth then nose. That stimulation causes the baby to take a deep breath and start to cry. Jim and Naomi join in with the crying. Keeping the baby at the same level as the uterus, we clamp the umbilical cord with both clamps and cut in between the clamps. We get a 1 minute assessment score and 5 minute assessment score on the newborn baby girl. We package both mom and baby up for safe transport and Trevor takes over. We advise Jim where to park when he gets to the hospital and the general direction of labor and delivery. While we are sure he knows where to go, his mind is on the new addition to their family and not necessarily on the task at hand.

"Man, you were great, Hardy. You were so calm and knew exactly what to do. I was shaking and couldn't believe it was happening!" Joey said as he sat next to me in the engine on our way back to the station. "You have done that before haven't you?"

"I have delivered a couple kids before. One thing is for sure, helping a new life come into this world never gets dull or boring." My mind goes back to when Wilma and Theo were born and I feel like I'm zoning out.

"Earth to Hardy. Earth to Hardy. You ok man?" Joey asked, looking concerned.

"Yeah, I'm fine. Just thinking." I reply.

"Nice job you two. You worked well together and were well prepared." Capt. Domingo says from the front of the engine. Wow, a rare compliment from the captain. This is going to be a good day I think to myself.

We get back to the public works building and continue on with our tasks of cleaning. After lunch, Joey and I head to the gym to lift weights. We push each other and complete circuit training to increase both our physical strength and cardiovascular strength.

After our workout session we decided to use the uniqueness of the public works garage to practice hose line stretches in a building we are unfamiliar with. The corners and obstacles create different challenges for us. We make a dinner of chicken fajitas, fried rice and beans and clean up the "kitchen". That evening, I relax on the couch with the next spy novel in the series I am reading.

I wake up in the morning after a restless night. It was busy with a couple fire alarms, a small grass fire from firework use, and several medicals. I am looking forward to the shift change and a couple hours rest at home. Our academy group decided to meet at the Silver Spur tonight for a get together.

I wake up from my nap feeling refreshed. I complete a couple of small chores before I head to the Silver Spur. I walk in and see Meredith, Lisa, and John. I head over to the table and take a seat.

"Hey guys, how's it going for you?" I am curious how their first few months have been going.

"It's going well. I like the crew I have been assigned. They never let me rest, but that is the life of a probie, I guess." Meredith says as she laughs.

"Amen to that!" Both Lisa and John agree.

"How's it going with you and Joey? At least you guys have each other to lean on." Lisa asks.

"Capt. Domingo has very high expectations. If you don't meet them, he has no qualms about telling you so in a very direct way." I laugh as I recall not being able to do anything right in his eyes. "He is very difficult to please.  I can see why nobody sticks around on his shift."  I am thankful Joey is with me.  It would be lonely without someone there to share in the bluntness that is Capt. Domingo."

"What about me?" Joey says as he approaches the table.

"We were asking how you and Hardy are surviving Capt. Domingo." Lisa says.

"He reminds me of the uncle no one likes.  He criticizes everything and you are never good enough to measure up to his impossible standard. Sound about right, Hardy?" Joey says

"Yeah, that is pretty accurate.  I just wonder why he is like that. Whippe, his engineer, sticks by him.  Whippe also told me not to judge a book by its cover and that Domingo has seen a few things in his career." I say, trying to defend the guy for some odd reason.  He gets on my nerves but what Whippe said to me has been rattling around in my head causing me to think.

The conversation moves on from Captain Domingo and onto our new fire station.  It is the talk of the department.  Everyone at the table is jealous that Joey and I get to work out of the new station.  I calmly remind everyone that it won't be functional until after the new staffing bid starts.

"Yeah, but no one will bid with Captain Domingo.  You will be working C shift Engine 2 unless there is another spot for you to bid." Meredith replies.

I quietly think to myself that even if I had a chance to bid away from Capt. Domingo, I might not.  Yes, he is demanding and has high expectations, but at the same time, I know what those expectations are.

I could take the chance and work for a captain that has random moving expectations, or one that doesn't care at all. No, I think to myself, Joey was wrong. Capt. Domingo isn't the crazy uncle. He is more the strict father type. Sometimes that is exactly what I need even when we disagree and challenge each other.

More of our cohort arrives and we hear their tales of the calls they went on and who they are working for. I was right, there could be worse than Capt. Domingo. Dan says the captain he works for is so erratic that every shift is like Russian roulette on the mood of the captain. On bad days, everyone runs and tries to hide to stay out of the line of fire.

After a couple more hours of conversation, we all head our separate ways. I head home and read for a while before heading off to bed. I am meeting with Sheila tomorrow for a check-in.

"Dylan, can you come to my office please?" Her boss says over the phone.

"On my way." Dylan replies wondering if this is about the Blue River Fire contract.

"Have a seat. How is it going with researching fire station designs?" He asks

"It is going well, there are so many different station designs that designing a unique station is almost the same as conforming to everyone else." She says with a laugh.

"Good, because the city council met, debated the proposals and we won the contract.  The Chief wants to get started next week.  Can you clear your Tuesday, Wednesday, and Thursday to interview all the firefighters? "

"Absolutely, it is already clear so I will just block those days so nothing gets added on." Dylan says while smiling. She can't believe she gets to design a fire station.  This will be so much fun she thinks to herself.

"Great.  I'll let you get back to your research.  I don't say it enough, but you have done great work here.  Keep it up." He finishes while turning back to his computer.

Smiling, she walks back to her office and dives back into her work.

I open the office door and hear the familiar dinging of the bell perched above.  Sheila looks up from her computer and smiles.

"Good morning, Hardy.  Have a seat and I'll be with you shortly. There is coffee if you would like."

"Thank you, Sheila." I say as I grab a cup of coffee. I sit down and thumb through a gardening magazine.

"So Hardy, it has been a little while.  How are things?" Sheila asks as she sits down.

"You know the usual up and down. Good days and bad days.  I did have a rollercoaster of emotions a little while back.  If it wasn't for Trevor, I don't know if I could have climbed out on my own." I say in blunt honesty.  Thinking back to the rescue and the depression that hit me full force the next day.

"Tell me about it, what happened?" she asks.

"Well, we were called to a house fire.  When we arrived, we found a mom and small child hanging their heads out of a second story window with the rooms and window filling with smoke.  Joey and I were able to rescue the kid first, then went to get mom and didn't see her. Joey climbed back up the ladder and found her unconscious on the bedroom floor. We were able to rescue her as well.  Both survived with no long term problems.  Capt. Domingo started screaming at us afterwards about how we were too slow, and we needed to do better next time.  When we got back to the station, I confronted Captain Domingo and told him that while there is always room to get better, we performed in an exceptional way and saved those lives." I pause to take a breath.

"Why do you think Capt. Domingo said that to you?" She asked, surprise evident on her face as she wrote down some notes.

"I honestly don't know. But Whippe, the engineer, came up to us afterwords and told us we did great.  Also, not to judge a book by its cover and that the captain has seen a lot in his career and this situation stressed him out." I responded back. "Then Trevor called that morning at shift change because he had heard about the rescue. He asked if I wanted to talk.  I said no.  I went home and fell asleep only to wake up from a nightmare accusing me of saving those two but not them and that I must not have loved them enough.  Then as I was staring at a picture of them, I kept putting their faces on the rescued victims in my mind and that spun me down the depression hole in a free fall.  Trevor broke into my house. Well, not really broke in, just found the spare key and let himself in. I guess he tried calling several times and I didn't answer. He even had my neighbor knock on the door. When no one could get hold of me, he left work and forced me out of bed. He said he wouldn't let me push him away again and that I am not going through this alone. Then he took me fishing. I was furious with him at first, but now I am grateful for him. That about sums it up. Oh, I forgot, I also helped deliver a baby girl last week." I finish while taking a deep breath.

"Oh, that is a lot to happen Hardy. How are you feeling about the rescue? Does anything change with your opinion on how it went.?"

"No, we executed a textbook rescue."

"From the situation you described, it seems very similar to the situation you went through. How are you with that?"

"It has been tough. I have had the devil and angel shoulder conversation already. While I wasn't there to save them, I was there to save the mother and child."

"That is a good way to look at it. And how about the baby delivery?"

"That is always an amazing thing to be a part of. I also was able to help Joey through his first delivery. Now that he has seen it done, he hopefully won't be shaking so much next time." I say with a laugh.

"I am glad you have reconnected with Trevor. It is good to have friends to help keep you on track. And he is right about judging other people. You don't know their story unless you ask and they are willing to tell you about it." She says rather cryptically. I mentally wonder what she means by that.

"Thank you, Sheila." We agreed on a day and time for our next check in. I leave feeling a little better than when I arrived, but I keep thinking about her comments about asking people about their story. What does that have to do with Captain Domingo I wonder to myself.

5

Dylan sets up her workstation in one of the corner offices of the public works building. She has received a lot of information from the first two days of interviewing the firefighters. She has already identified several common requests such as a commercial kitchen, individual bunks rooms, and a larger, more robust, gym. Surprisingly, the firefighters want a more traditional firehouse design with red brick versus steel and glass. She is starting to understand that traditions are huge in the fire service.

She consults her list and the first up is Captain Sal Domingo. She hears a knock on the door frame and looks up. She looks up and sees a tall man with salt and pepper hair. He looks like he is about 50 years old and has a large horseshoe moustache. He has piercing grey eyes that instantly prompt her to correct her posture. This man commands respect just by his presence she thinks to herself.

"Good morning, Capt. Domingo. Have a seat." She says sweetly, trying to get him to relax. "We have been contracted to design the new fire station number two. The fire chief has directed us to interview all current station two firefighters for design ideas and what you would like to see incorporated in its design."

"That's what I hear. For me I would like to see a large training area with movable walls, a forcible entry prop, a firefighter confidence course, and a roof prop. This would help me prepare these new kids coming in and increase their knowledge, skills, and abilities." Capt. Domingo says, crossing his arms over his chest.

"That's it? You don't have any suggestions for the rest of the building?" Dylan asks

"Well, not really. I liked the old station. Sure, it was old and falling down, but I don't need creature comforts. I am here to do a job and lead an engine company. I am close to retirement so I think the younger kids should have more of a say. Don't tell them I said that though. They think I am a demanding perfectionist, and I want it to stay that way." He says with a ghost of a smile on his face. Dylan starts to understand this captain. He is gruff on the outside, but he really cares about those he leads. He just shows it in a way that makes you want to be better and keep setting new goals to achieve throughout your career.

"OK, thank you for your input. I have had other requests for more training space. We will see what we can make work within the budget given." Dylan says while smiling back at him. Captain Domingo gets up and leaves the makeshift office.

"Knock knock." Says a male voice that belongs to a tall and

skinny man with blonde hair that has some grey in it. His face looks wrinkled, weathered, and tired. Dylan guesses he to be close to 60 years old.

"Hello, you must be Daryl Whippe. Nice to meet you. I am Dylan Arkham. We are gathering design ideas from those of you that will be working out of the new station two. I can't guarantee that everything you say here will be included but we are looking for themes and common ideas that we can include in the design while also staying within budget." Dylan says to Daryl as a greeting and icebreaker.

"Well, I would like an engineer's room for all of our spare equipment and toolboxes. I am the C shift engine FAO at station two. Part of our job is to make minor repairs of the engine and our equipment. It would be nice to have a tool room that can be organized and have an actual workbench to complete the repairs needed. I would also like separate bunk rooms. Some of these guys snore so loud you would think Zeus himself was throwing lightning and thunder down from Mount Olympus. Other than that, it doesn't matter to me. I plan on retiring within the next three years or so. I could retire now, but I enjoy what I am doing."

"So, this engineer's room, what would be in it? How many toolboxes, workbenches, cabinets, shelving? Also, how many square feet are you thinking?" Dylan is legitimately curious. No one has said anything about an engineer's room, however, the more she talks with Whippe, the more she can see why he is asking for one.

"I am thinking of 500 square feet with two toolboxes, two workbenches with cabinets along one wall, and shelving along another wall." Whippe says with a smile on his face.

"I'll admit, I am intrigued by this idea. I will see what I can make work, but I make no promise." Dylan says, trying to suppress a smile. "Thank you, have a wonderful rest of your shift." Whippe gets up and leaves.

Dylan takes a deep breath and gets up to get a glass of water before her next interview. She thinks back to the requests she has had so far. When she first received the project, she was thinking she was going to hear outlandish requests such as expensive recliners, big screen tv, a game room etc. The common perception is that firefighters sit around all day waiting for calls to come in. All the requests she has received either help them train better, keep their equipment in working order or help them be better rested and able to respond at a moment's notice. She makes a mental note to try to incorporate all of the requests into her design.

"Good afternoon, I'm Joey. I was told you wanted to meet with me?" Joey says as he flashes his smile and flexes his arms just a little bit.

"Nice to meet you Joey, I'm Dylan. I am the architect designing the new building. We are looking for firefighter input on the new design." Dylan smiles at him in a way that says nice try but not interested. Too young and cocky for me she thinks to herself. Then she chastised herself, ugh, why do I even care. I am here to do a job. Thanks, mom, for putting these thoughts in my head. She further scolds herself. She mentally shakes herself back to the present task at hand.

"Well, I want a better gym. We need to be physically fit, and our fitness area is so outdated. Also, can we get a patio with an outdoor gas fireplace? When I was on vacation in Aspen, I saw a fire station with an outdoor patio and gas fireplace. It looked like a cool place to gather in the evenings. Lastly, I was reading in a magazine about carcinogens, firefighters, and absorption. They said in the article that using a sauna after a fire can help push all the nasty stuff out of the pores and lessen our exposure. I think we need a sauna." He flashes his smile at Dylan again in an attempt to flirt.

"Is that all that is on your recommendation list?" Dylan says, trying to hide her laughter. She understands the gym as others have asked for a better gym as well. But for the others, Dylan feels like Joey wants things that look cool but maybe aren't really functional. "Well, thank you Joey, have a good rest of your shift." Dylan says in dismissal

"Thank you, Dylan, and you know where to find me if you have any more questions." Joey smiles at her again. There is always one Dylan thinks to herself as she realizes she just met the stereotypical firefighter that thinks they are God's gift to the world.

Ok, one more interview today and then I can compile everything and find the categories most requested. Before she starts on that she plans on relaxing on her couch with a good book and her favorite blanket to decompress. A knocking at the door frame jolts her out of her own head. "Excuse me, is this the right ro…" She looks up and stars into the most warm and comforting chocolate brown eyes she has ever seen. She sees those eyes widen in recognition just as she also recognizes those eyes. It's him, it's the guy from the Silver Spur, the one who held the door open for her, the same one she had noticed there a few times and couldn't stop staring at, until he would catch her and she would quickly look away.

He is even more intriguing up close. He is muscular but not fake gym muscular, more like a result of hard manual labor type job. A job like a firefighter, duh she thinks to herself that is why he is here. She realized he is still standing there as she has this internal monologue.

"Hardy Morrison? If that is you, then you are in the right place. Have a seat." Dylan says mustering as much confidence as she can. He doesn't say anything as he sits down. He keeps staring at her.

"You're the architect we are meeting?" He finally speaks and realizes how dumb it sounds.

"Yes, I am. I am Dylan. I am here to interview the firefighters about what they would like to see in the fire station design. Would you like to tell me what you would like in the station?" Dyan prompts

"I'm sorry, it's just your eyes look so familiar. I promise I am not hitting on you, I just have seen eyes like yours in several places around town, it caught me off guard. Yes, let's discuss the fire station design." Hardy says, trying to look away from the emerald green eyes staring back at him. "I would like a training area with training props. I may look older, but I am in my first year as a firefighter and need more practice. I would also like to see a commercial kitchen with a gas range, flat top grill, and a double oven. We are trying to eat healthier and cook a lot of lean protein, veggies, rice and salads. We also need a more robust gym space that can include both weight training and cardiovascular training spaces. Not all of us like to lift weights the entire time. We need to be functional and include working on our cardiovascular endurance. Separate sleeping quarters would be nice as some of the guy's here snore light freight trains. Other than that, I am just happy to be here and will be happy with whatever design you come up with." He finishes and works hard to avoid eye contact.

"Thank you Hardy, I really appreciate not only your suggestions but your reasons why. It helps me better understand the needs of the fire department. Here is my card, I really value your input, if you have any other suggestions please contact me." She hands over her business card. *What are you doing?* Her mind scolds her. *Seriously, you never give your card out in a nonprofessional setting. Don't kid yourself, you're hoping he calls for reasons other than the fire station design. Oh, be quiet,* she tells her own mind as she ends her inner monologue. She watches as Hardy leaves the room. She quickly gets up and shuts the door,

"Oh my" she says out loud as she starts fanning herself. She takes a deep breath as she tries to calm her racing heart. There is something interesting about him that draws her in. Those chocolate brown eyes are going to haunt her dreams tonight. She just knows it. After her heart calms down, she packs up her papers and computer and quickly leaves the building for her car to head home.

I leave the office and go to the washroom to splash some water on my face. OH MY GOD…. IT'S HER, the woman I have seen staring at me at the Silver Spur and in the office of Structural Design Architect Group when I was out for my run., my mind screams at me. I need to calm my racing heart. Sure, she is attractive. I can appreciate that. Plus, her eyes are a stunning emerald green. That's why I am having this reaction, because of her eyes, I try to convince myself. I stare in the mirror. "You come with a lot of baggage and are hurt. She doesn't need that. Sure, it seems like she was flirting but you are better off alone. Don't give your heart a chance to be shattered again." I tell my reflection in the mirror. With my resolve back, I crumple up her business card in my fist and throw it away in the trash can. Taking a few more deep breaths, I make sure I project calm and leave the washroom to continue my daily duties.

My shift continues on, like any other shift. We have a training session, we spend some time on physical fitness, and we respond to calls. The only difference is those emerald green eyes were constantly on my mind. The dinner conversation revolved around the new station, design ideas and what everyone wanted to see incorporated. From the sounds of it, a new kitchen, and individual bunks rooms were on the top of everyone's list.

After dinner cleanup is complete, I curl up on a chair and grab the latest spy novel I rented from the library. Maybe a good spy novel will take my mind off of Dylan. That name seems to fit her feisty take charge personality. I laugh as I recall Joey coming out of his meeting complaining about "the architect girl" not acknowledging his flirting attempts.

BEEP BEEP BEEP Engine 2, Ladder 2 motor vehicle crash Newberry lane and High Cross Street. Everyone jumps out of their chairs and moves to the apparatus bay to gear up and respond.

Both the ladder truck and engine navigate the heavy traffic as they approach the crash. They position their apparatus to block traffic and create a somewhat safe work area. Working in traffic is never completely safe. Traffic is like water; if they find a small opening, they will flow through it. Capt. Domingo takes command and assigns the ladder to extrication and the engine to patient assessment. A scene size up on approach reveals a three-vehicle accident with a midsized blue SUV with heavy damage rolled over and resting on the passenger side. The driver appeared to still be in the vehicle. The other two vehicles had moderate damage, and the drivers were still in their vehicles, and we could see them moving around. Joey goes to the red two door passenger car, and I go to the 4-door black pickup truck.

I approach the truck "Hello sir, I'm Hardy and I am with the fire department. What is your name?"

"My name is Tom Lanford." The male driver says with a grimace.

"It looks like you're in pain. Where do you hurt?"

"My chest hurts. That car came out of nowhere sideswiped me, side swiped the other car and then rolled. Scared the crap out of me."

"Were you wearing your seatbelt? Did you hit your chest on anything? Did you lose consciousness?"

"I was wearing my seatbelt, I didn't hit anything, and unfortunately I remember everything."

Sense of humor is intact, I think to myself. "Ok, does it hurt to take a deep breath?" I ask as I hook him up to our monitor to look at his heart rate, heart rhythm, blood pressure, and oxygen saturation.

"No, it hurts when I move or press on my chest."

I look at his vital signs. His heart rate is slightly elevated, along with his blood pressure. I expected that after what he just went through. His heart rate is sinus tach. I do not see any ST segment elevation, or depression, I lit up his shirt and see the imprint of the seat belt across his chest. "Ok, I don't see any life-threatening injuries. I am going to go check on the other drivers and I'll be back to check on you, OK?"

"Ok, thank you Hardy." Tom replies as he closes his eyes and takes a deep breath.

I look over at Joey and he waves me away. I head over to the rolled over vehicle and see Ladder 2 has the vehicle stabilized and is cutting around the driver to remove them from the car. I ask the ladder captain if the driver is conscious and if there are any injuries that they know of. The ladder captain tells me they can smell an odor of alcohol coming from the car and that the driver is responding to them with slurred speech and is confused. While this appears to be an intoxicated driver that caused this crash, we need to evaluate the driver for a possible stroke, hypoglycemia, seizure, or illicit substance ingestion. All could possibly have caused this crash. We cannot jump to conclusions.

With the patient boarded and removed from the car, I check his blood sugar. It is normal. Blood pressure is normal; heart rate is slower than normal. Oxygen saturation is 88% on room air. The patient is breathing on their own, but the respiratory rate is low. We assist breathing with a bag valve mask and supplemental oxygen. He is going to the hospital to be further evaluated but more than likely he is just extremely intoxicated.

Lime County EMS arrives, and we give patient care reports for all three drivers. The drivers of the other two vehicles refuse transport to the hospital. We packed up our equipment and returned to our temporary station. As we pulled in the bay, Cpt. Domingo turned around and stared at me. "Morrison, see me in my office." He then exited the engine and walked off down the hallway.

"Good luck Morrison." Whitman whispers without making eye contact. Oh man, what did I do now, I think to myself.

I knock on the captain's door. "Come in." A gruff and irritated voice replies.

"Sir, you wanted to see me?" I say in as neutral of a voice as I can.

"Take a seat." He stares at me with unblinking eyes. "You seem distracted today. You weren't yourself and on that last call, you were standing next to the overturned car talking with the ladder captain while they were performing extrication and you did not have your protective gear on. That can't happen again. Do you want to talk about what has distracted you?

"I'm sorry sir. That won't happen again. I didn't think I was that close, and I was asking the ladder captain about the status of the driver, so I knew what to prepare for once he was extricated. I have nothing that I want to talk about." I say as the staring contest continues.

"Dismissed." He says after a very long time.

I get up and leave without a word. As I walk away, I now understand why many people think the crusty old timer needs to retire. I know I wasn't too close to the car, and I was doing my job. I'm not sure why he is singling me out and being petty, but it is getting really annoying.

As Morrison leaves the office, Capt. Domingo wonders to himself if he is being too hard on him. No, he resolves, Morrison has a lot of potential, but he needs discipline. He sees a lot of himself in Morrison when he was that age.  Plus, he knows what Morrison went through, and he is pretty sure that is what has distracted him.  He wishes Morrsion would open up about it.  He wants to talk about that night but wants Morrsion to start the conversation.

# 6

Dylan is working on the design of the new station and trying to incorporate as many of the wants and requests from the line staff. The trouble is that the vision of chocolate eyes keep distracting her. Not only that, but her attempt at flirting also apparently fell flat as Hardy had not called her. "What did you expect? You don't date, and you never initiate the conversation. You always wait for someone to ask and just go for something to do." She mumbles to herself. "Why do I feel drawn to him? I don't have time to date, yet my stomach flutters every time I see him. It happened when he opened the door at the Silver Spur, and the several times I had caught a glimpse of him the couple other times I went there, then my stomach was doing full on back flips during our station design meeting. AAAGGGHH!!!!!

She sets her project aside and thinks about all the chance

encounters she has had with Hardy. She wonders why she is drawn to him and why she reacts the way she does. She wants to find out why so she decides to leave her comfort zone and explore whatever this is. She thinks about how she can see him again without looking desperate. She decides to show up at the station at shift change and ask to meet again as she has more questions. It isn't a lie, she does have questions, just not about the fire station design. Frustrated and unable to focus on her work, she grabs her gym bag, and heads to the restroom to change into her running clothes. A good run is just what she needs to clear her head. She puts her ear buds in and starts her music playlist for long runs.

She finishes her run back in front of the office and stops and doubles over trying to catch her breath. She clearly had a lot on her mind. She ran 13 miles and completely lost track of time. She doesn't even bother going back up to her office. She climbs in her car and heads home. She is looking forward to her dinner and then a date on her couch with her favorite book and blanket.

She makes herself a dinner of chicken parm, with a side of Caesar salad and a couple of breadsticks. This is her go to comfort meal after a long run. She spent three hours reading her latest western romance novel and loved to live vicariously through the characters in the books. Feeling content, she heads upstairs and falls asleep.

Dylan wakes up a nervous ball of energy. She gets dressed, eats a small breakfast of a yogurt cup and coffee in an attempt to settle her stomach. She grabs her keys and drives to the public works building before she talks herself out of her plan. "What am I doing?" She asks out loud to no one in particular during her drive over. She pulls into the parking lot and parks next to Hardy's truck. She listens to the radio while she waits for him to come out

The door opens and Hardy walks out. Dylan feels her heart rate increase and her stomach starts to summersault. Her breath catches as she makes eye contact with him. He stops in his tracks and just stares at her mouth hanging partially open. He breaks eye contact and starts walking to his truck. When he gets between the vehicles she rolls her window down. "Hi Hardy."

"Hi Dylan. You have another meeting today?"

"Well, I hope so. I have some questions, and I was hoping you have some answers for me. Are you free? She says with a hopeful smile on her face.

"You have questions for me? Right now? Umm…sure. Shall we head back inside?

"Actually, I know of a good cafe down the road, and I haven't had breakfast. Care to join me and we can talk over breakfast?

There is a long awkward pause, and she can almost see the internal debate raging in his head. She gets nervous thinking he is going to decline.

"Sure, I am kind of hungry. It's not like it is a date." He says quietly, almost to himself.

For some reason, that hurts worse than a rejection. Dylan puts a smile on her face to hide her disappointment. "Ok, it's Jimmy's Cafe down on main street. Follow me there?"

"I know the place, lead the way." He gives her a big smile.

On the drive over to the cafe, Dylan frantically tries to come up with questions related to the station design.  She realizes she must ask some design related questions, or he is going to think this is a date.

They arrive at the cafe and Hardy holds the door open for Dylan. They are seated in a corner booth. Neither look at the menu as the waitress arrives.

"Hello, I'm Becky. What can I get you to drink?

"Coffee and a water please" Dylan says

"Same for me" Hardy replies

The waitress leaves to grab the coffee and water.  "Do you know what you want? Dylan asks?

"Yes, how about you?" Hardy replies

"Yes, I'm getting my usual."

The waitress returns with the coffee and water.  "Are you ready to order?

"Yes, we are.  I'll have the country omelet with pancakes please." Dylan replies, handing her menu to the waitress.

"I'll have the same.  Thank you." Hardy replies while staring and smiling at Dylan.  "You don't strike me as the omelet and pancake type."

"Oh, I grew up on a ranch in Montana.  A big breakfast was a necessity because many times you wouldn't eat again until later that evening."

"I never would have guessed.  So, what questions do you have for me?"

"I'm struggling with the size of the gym. How much space does the gym need?

"I would say as big as it can be.  There are nine of us on shift so it can get pretty busy."

"How long have you been with Blue River Fire?"

"I'm on my probationary year. I finished the academy earlier this year. Why?"

"Oh, really? You had a lot of great ideas. I figured you had been on for a while."

"Nope, I'm a probie.  How about you?  How long have you been an architect?

"I have been an architect for a little over a year.  This is the first company I have worked for. I love it so far.  I have never designed a fire station before.  It is a challenge that I have been enjoying.  What about you? What did you do before joining the fire department?"

She saw his eyebrows pinch together and he looked to be thinking.  There was a long awkward pause.

"I worked in landscaping and that left me feeling unfulfilled. So, I changed careers."

She had the feeling there was more to the story, but she didn't want to press the issue.  The more she talks with him, the more intrigued she is.

The food arrives and they eat in silence for a few minutes.

"So, how do you like working for the fire department?" Dylan asks between bites breaking the silence.

"It is fun. No day is ever the same and we get to help people who are sick or need rescue or just generally solve a problem for them.  There is a downside to the job, there are times where we witness firsthand, some of the most horrific things people can do to each other, or seeing families absolutely heartbroken over loss of a home or family members. The positives far outnumber the negatives but it's the negatives that tend to stay with you and the memories can pop up out of nowhere and at the most inconvenient times. Or something that happens can trigger a negative memory and cause depression and a stress reaction. PTSD is real and can be absolutely devastating if it isn't acknowledged or managed. I'm sorry that was kind of depressing, makes you want to apply to be a firefighter doesn't it." Hardy says with a laugh to lighten the mood. "What about you? Why architecture?

"Well, I liked to draw and design as a kid. I started drawing and designing buildings in middle school for fun. I knew I didn't want to be a rancher. Don't get me wrong, I love the outdoors, but I didn't love the ranching business. I loved math, drawing, and designing while I was in school. Architect seemed like a natural fit. It is tough though. It took me a while to get this job. But I like challenges and when people tell me no, it causes me to work harder to prove myself."

Dylan looks at her watch and realizes it is almost 11am. "Oh my, I need to get back to the office. I really enjoyed our talk. You are very interesting Hardy. We should do this again."

"I agree it was fun. You are really interesting, but I am not looking for a relationship. I have things I am working through and dealing with. I know it sounds cliche but it's not you, it really is me. I am not good company long term. You're a great person, I can tell that from talking with you, you deserve better than me." Hardy says with sadness filling his eyes.

Dylan wonders what put that sadness there. Something

happened to him she thinks to herself. Yep, she was right, there is more to his story than he is letting on. "I'm sorry if I gave you the wrong impression, Hardy. I'm not looking for a relationship either. I just want to get to know you better. There is nothing wrong being friends and meeting for coffee occasionally is there?" She stares at him as he looks back at her clearly thinking it through.

"No, I guess not. Let me think about it. I mean it when I say I have a past that I am working through and it is a struggle."

With that Hardy pays the bill much to Dylan's protest. "I'm sorry, I can't let you pay this time. If there is another time, you can pay. Deal?" Hardy asks her, eyebrow raised.

"Ok, you win this time. You have my number, call me if you would like to chat over coffee."

With that Dylan stood up and walked to her car to go to her office. Hardy stayed in the booth sipping his coffee.

"Ok, that didn't go as I planned. But like I told him, I like challenges. It is clear he has built up a wall around him. It is clear he is miserable outside of work." she says to herself as she reaches her car. Even if he isn't interested in her, she wants to be a good friend and help him break through.

I sit in my booth replaying the conversation in my head. What just happened. It felt like a date. I thought she had questions about the station design; however, we ended up talking about our histories. I am not doing this. I cannot open up again. The pain of loss will destroy me. I like her and she is intriguing, but I am no good for her. I need to focus on my job, that has been the one steady thing that has helped me move forward. I leave the cafe and head home.

The morning is still playing back in my mind, and I can't focus and feel very restless. I decided to grab my archery gear and go to a 3D shooting range. It is a fun outdoor course that is pseudo hunting. In this range, you follow a course and shoot at 3D targets of deer, turkey, bear, etc. It feels like real hunting where you shoot at life sized targets.

I walk down the first trail letting the warm sun wash over me and the birds chirping to calm my racing mind. I round the first bend and find a tom standing on the edge. I pull the string back as I raise my bow and sight in the turkey. Taking a deep breath, I slowly let it out as I released the string watching the arrow fly straight and true, hitting its mark. I walk up to the turkey and retrieve my arrow. I close my eyes and take a deep breath. I can feel the tension leaving my body. I spend the next three hours walking the course and shooting various targets along the trail. As I finish the course, I feel much more relaxed with a clearer focus.

Back at my truck, I grab my cell phone and see a missed call from Trevor. He left a voicemail and is wondering if I would like to go fishing. I call him back and we decide to meet at the boat launch in an hour. I head back home to drop off my archery equipment and grab my fishing equipment.

I meet Trevor at the boat launch and help him with the boat. We push away from the dock and head down the river. We arrive at our normal fishing spot, and he cuts the engine letting the current take over. We cast our lines and sit in comfortable silence for a few minutes.

"How have you been, Hardy" Trevor says as an icebreaker.

"I'm doing ok. I haven't had a nightmare in a while so I'm thankful for that. I am rediscovering my hobbies and how much they calm my mind. Thankfully I have hobbies that I enjoy. I couldn't imagine trying to get my life back together if I had nothing to enjoy. I'm just beginning to realize how far I fell down the PTSD hole I fell."

"I'm glad to hear you recognize not only how far you were down but also how much progress you have made. There are a lot of people here cheering you on and willing to help. All you need to do is ask."

"Asking for help is hard. We are the ones normally solving problems for everyone else. To admit you need help feels like failure."

"And that right there is the mentality that needs to change in public safety. We are not superhuman. We are just as fallible as those we help. Let me ask you one question. "When you help someone solve a problem, be it a medical, fire, or other problem, do you think less of them?

"NO. I am happy to help them and have a sense of pride and accomplishment afterward."

"Ok, it is the exact same feeling for those who work to help us. Do you understand what I am saying? Let them help."

"I hear what you're saying."

"Ok, now that the heavy talk is over. What's this I hear about your date with the architect?"

"What date!?" I choke out through mid-drink of my iced tea. "There was no date. She had more questions about the fire station design."

"That's not what Joey is saying. He saw you leave with her from the station parking lot after a shift. He also said she has not had another meeting with any other firefighter."

"I promise you, it was no date. We talked about the station design over breakfast."

"Right. No date." Trevor eyes me suspiciously. "You met in a public place, shared a meal and conversation with an attractive single woman around your age. Sounds like a first date to me. There is nothing wrong with it, Hardy. I say go for it!"

"First, it was NOT a date. Second, this part of the conversation is over!" I say while trying not to laugh.

"Ok, if you say so."

7

Dylann struggles at her computer as she works on the station design. Frustrated, she stands up and walks around her office. On any given project, she can focus and work for hours uninterrupted. Not on this project. Her mind is getting in the way. Hardy Morrison has completely taken up residence in her thoughts. Looking into his eyes during that breakfast last week felt like coming home. She knows he is going through something. She can see it in his body language. She would like to help him through it. She knows there is a good and gentle person on the inside. She hasn't felt like this about a man ever. It is both scary and exciting. She wants to be in his life, even if it is only friends.

She decides to go for a run to clear her head. She grabs her gym back and goes to change into running clothes. Leaving Structural Designs, she starts running. Earbuds in place and listening to her favorite

90s country hits, she lets the miles pile on and her mind clear out. She didn't have a specific route planned out but clearly her feet knew where they wanted to go as she realized she was approaching the public works building/ makeshift fire station.

As she approaches, she wonders if Hardy is working. Well, so much for this run distracting her. Then she sees him. He is working out with Joey. He is jumping rope while Joey is lifting a kettlebell. She watches them as she keeps running. She sees his arm and leg muscles flexing as he jumps rope and it puts her in a trance. She sees the sweat dripping down and realizes he is one gorgeous man. Joey is good looking as well, but he looks like a boy next to Hardy. Feeling suddenly short of breath, she stops running at the same moment Joey smacks Hardy and the arm and points her direction.

"Hey Dylan, you don't look so well. Are you ok?" Joey yells as he comes over with Hardy right on his heels.

"I'm fine. Just catching my breath from my run" Dyan lies and catches just a little smirk from Hardy.

"Well, you are flushed with a rapid heart rate." Hardy says as he grabs her wrist and then quickly let's go with wide eyes.

Yup, he felt it as well, Dylan thinks to herself. She felt the same thing as soon as his fingers touched her wrist. She would like to feel it again and again.

"I just ran a little farther and harder than I normally run. I'll be fine in a few minutes. I promise." Dylan says with more confidence. "See my heart rate is slowing down" and holds out her wrist to Hardy.

He touches her wrist again and she immediately feels the

wonderful electricity flowing. She tries not to smile as Hardy holds on for a little longer this time.

"Are you sure you're ok? Would you like a ride to wherever you are going? "Hardy asks with concern in his voice.

"I will be fine. I am heading back to my office to continue the design. "Dylan says while smiling at Hardy.

"OK, here is my number. Please call me when you make it back. So, I don't worry you have collapsed somewhere between here and there." Hardy says while writing down his number on a scrap piece of paper and handing it to her. "If I don't hear from you in two hours, we may have to send a search party. Your office is 6 miles from here. You should be back within two hours."

"I will call you when I get back. I promise" Dylan says, unable to suppress the smile from forming.

As Dylan starts walking away, she hears Joey mutter "It wasn't a date huh. She is totally into you. You would be stupid not to go out with her. I'm actually jealous of you old man." and then she hears "Enough Joey, there are things you just can't understand." Now that she is too far away to hear any more conversation she does a happy dance in her head. She got his number. That wasn't the goal of this run but she will take what the good Lord gives her.

She does a half walk and half jog on the way back. Her mind is now surprisingly clear. He has that effect on her. Too bad it doesn't last long and she needs another dose. Oh boy, she has it bad. Thinking about the request to contact him, should she send a text, or should she make a voice call? She weighs the pros and cons and decides she wants to hear his voice. It is more personal. She has also decided she will get coffee and bagel sandwiches and meet him at the station in the morning. She really wants to talk to him about this connection that after today, she knows they both feel.

She arrives back at her office in one hour and fifteen minutes. She climbs the stairs to her office and grabs her cell phone. She pulls out the piece of paper with his number and stares at it. Hands shaking, she starts dialing his phone number one slow agonizing button at a time. Of all the times, why has her mind decided now is the time to go blank and lose focus. The line starts ringing and she freezes, unable to speak and her stomach in knots.

"Ok, Joey. You have had your fun. She is very attractive, but I am a mess inside and she doesn't need that in her life. Let's get back to our workout."

"But Hardy, she totally has eyes for you. And even I can see the way you look at her. You are going to let that go? No, you need to see where a relationship with her goes. Trust me, I'm not into long term, but even I can see that you both have long term together written all over your faces." Joey says as he picks up the jump rope and I switch to the kettlebell.

After 30 minutes, we finish our workout, shower and change back into our uniforms. We need to get ready for a fire safety talk at the elementary school in an hour. I am reviewing the material we are presenting when my phone rings. It is Dylan, I had already programmed her number into my contact list when I ran back to the garbage can and grabbed her business car out of it. I quietly sneak outside so I can speak without being hounded by Joey.

"Hey Dylan, did you make it back safe?" I ask, already knowing the answer. After a short while there was still silence on the other end.

"Dylan, are you there?" Panic started to creep in my voice. Still Silence.

"If you can hear me hit a button." I say trying to triage the severity of what's going on.

"I'm Sorry Hardy. My brain locked up. I think it was nerves. Oops. Umm, did I say that last part out loud?" Dylan says and I can hear her face contort in her voice.

"Yes, you did say that last part out loud." I reply with a chuckle in my voice. "Are you back at your office?"

"Yes, I am back and slightly embarrassed. So, would you be mad if I brought you a coffee and breakfast sandwich in the morning? I want to walk and talk with you because I have questions about this connection between us. I know you feel it as well. I want to hear your take on it." Dylan says in a rush.

Great, now it's my brain's turn to freeze.

"Hardy are you still there?" Dylan says with panic in her voice.

"Yes, sorry, my brain decided to not work. I would like that very much, but I don't know how helpful I will be." I say as I hear the beeps for a call in the background.

"I'm sorry I must go. We are being dispatched to a call."

We are responding to a possible apartment fire. Capt. Domingo updates us that there is a confirmed apartment fire on the first floor and that we will be the second arriving engine. As we arrive, command tasks us with pulling a line off our engine and making our way to the second floor for primary search and checking for fire extension. Capt. Domingo scouts quickly while Joey and I start deploying hose.

"6 sections. Hurry up! You're moving too slow!" Capt. Domingo yells at us.

We estimate we need 100 feet of skid load to the entry door, 50 feet for the stairwell, and another 150 to make our way down the hallway on the second floor. Joey grabs the bundle and two 50 foot loops, I grab another two 50 foot loops and as we step away from the truck, Daryl , pulls another two sections off the engine and connects it to the discharge. Joey and I start walking in tandem.

"Move with Purpose!  Fireground Pace! Let's go!" Barks Capt. Domingo.

We are hustling.  I don't know why he is pissed but he is starting to piss me off.  Now I understand why many people think he just needs to retire.

We get close to the entry door and the bundle on my left shoulder starts to flank out.  We get to the second-floor landing and I crack the door and see it is a dirty hallway with lots of smoke.  We decide to flank the rest of the hose in the stairwell.  I take the 50-foot section from Joey's left shoulder, along with the 50 foot section from my right shoulder and start walking up to the third floor landing.  With our line laid out nicely we call for water.

Our line ready, we mask up and start working our way down the hallway searching apartments for people, smoke, and fire. Joey is on the nozzle, and I am backing him up. When we come to a door, we open it or force it open. He will stay at the door while I enter the room and complete a quick search for people or fire.

We move efficiently while also being thorough, so we don't miss anyone. In the meantime, Capt. Domingo is still barking at us to move quicker. He and I are going to have words after this. He needs to chill out. We are reaching the unit that is right above the fire apartment, when someone across the hall opens their apartment door and coughs. We tell them to get back inside their apartment and go to the window.

Capt. Domingo calls our division officer on the radio and advises of a person needing assistance getting out through a window on the Charlie side second floor towards the Charlie/Delta corner.

We open the door and are met with thicker smoke and more heat. We start searching for the source. We search the kitchen, bedrooms and living room and are unable to locate the fire. We know it is here somewhere. We need to be able to find it.

"Wasn't it a kitchen fire downstairs?" Joey asks after a short while.

"Yes, contained in the kitchen." Capt. Domingo replies.

"I know I am young and inexperienced, but if the fire downstairs was contained to the kitchen, should we be focusing on checking for extensions directly above. In this kitchen?" Joey says with a slight smile on his face.

I can tell he is irritated with Capt. Domingo as well.

Without saying a word, Captain Domingo walks towards the kitchen yelling out orders to move the fridge and oven unit out and away from the walls. Joey and I move the oven first and I smile.

"Nice job Joey. You called it." I say with pride in my voice.

He just nods as we see the smoldering embers of a fire right where the floor and wall meet. Joey goes to grab the nozzle while I start tearing the gypsum board away from the wall to find how much hidden fire there is in the concealed space.

We expose and extinguish all the fire until we have clean unburned wood all around the burned area. We are sure we have the fire out, Capt. Domingo radios to the division boss that we found extension, have it extinguished, and have completed overhaul, then we leave to recycle. Recycle is where we leave the hazard zone, get a new bottle of air placed in our SCBA packs, grab a quick bottle of water and wait for another assignment.

Our next assignment is to conduct a secondary search, ensure the fire is out and conduct more overhaul if needed in the primary fire unit. We use our thermal imaging camera (TIC) and check for heat signatures. We also use our New York hooks to poke inspection holes checking for hidden fire in the concealed spaces. We also complete a more thorough search looking for people that may have been missed during the primary search.

As much as we don't like it, people can be missed, especially if they are already deceased, during the initial search and primary control because crews are more focused on eliminating the threat (putting the fire out) and many times starting running low on air and need to leave the hazard. Then the replacement crew to finish the initial task may think an area was already searched or not search an area before they need to leave. That is why our policy here in Blue River is to send a different crew to complete a secondary search as an insurance policy. We do not find any people or fire and leave the hazard zone.

We are released from the scene and pack up our equipment. The ride back is quiet. Upon our return. Capt. Domingo, Joey and I shower to rid our bodies from as many carcinogens as possible and change into clean uniforms. We then go out and help Daryl rack new hose on our engine. We then put our back up turnout gear on the engine. With our apparatus back in working order, we start washing and scrubbing the hose used as well as our SCBAs. With the hose and SCBAs taken care of we put our dirty turnouts in the extractor to wash. The extractor is a special washing machine that helps pull most of the carcinogens out of our gear.

I decide to talk with Capt. Domingo about him yelling at us for no reason. I make my way to his office where he is completing paperwork from the fire.

"Hey Capt. You have a moment?" I ask as nicely as I can

"Yea, what do you need Morrison?" He grumbles as he looks away from his monitor and takes his hands off the keyboard.

"Can you explain why you were yelling at us to move quicker? Joey and I were moving very fast and deployed the line without issue. I guess I don't understand what more you want."

"That smoke looked bad, and we needed to get in there and make rescues before it was too late.  It did not look like you were moving very fast." He says, staring at me.

"That is a load of crap, and you know it.  Joey and I were moving as fast as we could deploying the skid load with only the two of us.  To be honest, you looked distracted.  I've heard from others that you should retire and that you ride people too hard.  I am beginning to understand why they say that. It seems to me you are too focused on speed and not enough on smooth efficiency."

Capt. Domingo is silent for so long I start to get nervous.

"Close the door Morrison and have a seat." He says so quietly I almost didn't hear him.

I close the door, sit down and stare at him.

"I was there." he says in a whisper.

"You were where, sir?"

"I was at your house, the night your family died." He looks up and a tear is trying to escape his left eye.

My mouth opens, then closes, then opens, then closes.  I am unable to speak.

"I was the captain of the first due engine.  We arrived and tried to make a rescue, but we were too late.  We didn't make it in time. The conditions were so bad we couldn't make the rescues.  Ever since then, I have been drilling my crews about speed AND efficiency.  I'm so sorry Hardy.  I have carried that guilt with my every day since then"

Suddenly recognition hits me like a brick to the face.  That is where I recognize him from.

"That was you sitting on the back of the engine trying not to cry, wasn't it." I say fighting back my own tears.

"Yeah, I saw you pull up in an ambulance and I first thought you were there in a work capacity.  Then I heard it was your house and your family.  The realization that you were one of us and just lost your family hit me hard.  I had just buried my dear Rosalie two weeks prior, so I knew the pain you were going through and I just broke down." He says through tears now freely flowing.

"So, you knew my history while I was in the academy."  I blurt out.

"Yes, at first, I was skeptical about your invitation to the academy. But your grit, determination, and resolve impressed me.  That is why I have such high demands on those that work with me. I don't ever want to be in that position again thinking we could have moved faster and prevented a death." He says with more conviction.

"The coroner report says they died of carbon monoxide poisoning. They were dead before the fire reached them, before you guys even arrived.  It wasn't your fault." I try to reassure him.

"I did not hear that.  That helps ease the guilt a little bit.  I can't get the picture of them huddled together on the floor below the window out of my memories.  I heard that you felt responsible.  Why do you feel responsible? You were at work providing for them.  That I don't understand."

"I was the one that left the propane tanks under the service mast for the power lines right next to the glass patio door.  If those hadn't been there, the fire would not have grown so fast and cut off their only escape route (other than jumping out of the window).  Plus, I did not have an escape ladder in that bedroom. I had been meaning to get one, just never got around to it. While I did not start the fire, it was my lack of attention to detail that contributed to their deaths."

"I see. From the fire investigation report, it was the open doors, windows and wind speed and direction that created a flow path and funnel for the fire to grow rapidly and cut off the stairs. Those were all circumstances out of either of our control." He counters.

"I know, I read the report. I still feel responsible."

"Let's make a deal. We both need to stop holding ourselves hostage over things we can't control. I know a really good therapist that has helped me with both personal stress and professional stress. Can I recommend her?"

"That's nice of you to offer, but I already see a therapist. Her name is Sheila, and she is really good." I say with a hint of pride in my voice. Capt. Domingo just stares at me.

"Now it makes a lot more sense. That is who I was going to recommend. I see her on a regular basis. Would you be interested in a joint session with Sheila to talk about this incident knowing we were both so invested in it?" He asks with hopefulness in his voice.

I think that is a great idea. Thank you, Capt., for this. I recognized you from academy day one, but I couldn't place where I knew you from. Now I know. For the record, I like working for you. I just wish you would stop riding Joey and I so hard." I say laughing a little.

"It is my job to help you reach your full potential and be the best. I won't relax my standards but maybe now that you know why, it won't bother you so much. Just one thing."

"What is it?"

"Can we keep that between us? I like that people think I am a crusty old codger. If word got out, I will really have to start increasing my motivation strategies. If these young kids can't handle a little pressure and motivation, I don't want them on my engine." He smiles at me.

"You got it." I say and make a zip my lips motion.

The next morning, Dylan waits in line at the local family-owned coffee shop and tries to calm her nerves. She rubs her hands up and down her pants in an attempt to rid the sweat from her palms. This is new territory for her, she has never been nervous over a man before. "Calm down Dylan, it's just a talk with a friend." She quietly says to herself. She knows it is a lie, she feels like they have more to offer each other.

"Hi, what can I get for you?" the perky cashier asks.

"May I order two large dark roasts, black, and two sausage, egg, and cheese breakfast muffins please." Dylan replies with a smile on her face.

"Absolutely, your order will be ready at the other end of the counter. "

"Thank you."

Dylan grabs her order and steps outside. She looks at her watch and sees she has 30 minutes until shift change. The station is a 20-minute walk away.  It is a gorgeous morning with the sun shining brightly and a slight breeze in the air.  She decides to walk to the station.  The walk helps build her confidence.  She arrives at the makeshift station and sits down at a picnic table near the entrance.  As she waits, all of her confidence seems to seep out of her body as her hands fidget in her lap.

She felt his gaze before she actually saw him.  She looked up and saw uneasiness in his eyes.  Her stomach felt like it was on a rollercoaster.  She was unsure if he had a bad night or if it was her presence that has that look in his eyes.

"I'm sorry, I've had an emotional night.  I see that inner monologue in your head.  I promise , it is not you that has this look on my face." He prompts as he approaches.  She sends up a silent prayer of thanks.

"Do you want to talk about it?" Dylan asks hopefully using that as a conversation starter.

"I'm not ready to talk about details but I learned something last night that changes my perspective on both past and present events." He says cryptically

"Ok, I brought breakfast. Do you want to eat here, then go for a walk?" Dylan says while holding the bag of sandwiches and coffee.

"That smells amazing.  Yes, let's eat here.  Then we can walk and drink our coffee."

Hardy sits down across from Dylan, and she hands him a sandwich and coffee.  They sit in silence for a few minutes as they eat and steal looks at each other when they think the other isn't looking.

"So, how was your shift yesterday?

"It was steady.  We had a handful of medicals, a couple of fire alarms, and an apartment fire.  I'm looking forward to a couple of days off so I can work on some house projects."

"What house projects are you working on?"

"I am re-building the deck, and I want to build a storage shed in the backyard."

"That sounds like fun.  Do you like building things?"

"Yes, it keeps my mind occupied and keeps me engaged in the present."

Dylan files that information away in the back of her head.  He clearly has something in his past, but he is not ready to talk about it yet. "Ready to go for a walk?"

"Yes ma'am.  Lead the way." Hardy says as he stands up and holds his arm out.

They start walking down main street and into the center of town. They are headed towards the park on the bank of the blue river.  There is a nice walking path that follows the river for a way.  Dylan uses the silence to figure out how to start the conversation she really wants to have.  She keeps thinking of opening lines and then immediately dismisses them as too cheesy.  She is so lost in her head she doesn't notice Hardy stealing glances at her and studying her facial expressions.

"Penny for your thoughts?" Hardy says, bringing Dylan back to the here and now.

"I'm sorry, I was thinking of how to start the conversation but hadn't been able to come up with anything that wasn't cheesy or typical. I guess I'll just come out with it.  I feel this attraction between us, and I think you do too. Do you feel it? Or am I just crazy?" Dylan looks at Hardy for confirmation.

"Yeah, I feel it. Honestly, it scares me to death. I've told you I have a past. It has a lot of heartache, despair, and emotions I would rather not revisit. You're beautiful, smart, funny and a joy to be around. I'm afraid I will only bring clouds and rain to your sunny disposition. I vowed to not get close to anyone ever again because I'm not sure I could survive that kind of heartache again. I don't want to be a downer, but I feel I owe you an honest answer. I am a mess, and I am slowly trying to rebuild my life."

"I appreciate the honesty. What makes you so sure you would bring clouds and rain?

"Because every day is a battle. Some days it's a battle to get out of bed. Some days it's a battle to be around happy people. Some days it's a battle to not feel bad when you're having a good day. And some nights, nightmares chase the sleep away."

"Hardy, I feel like our paths are crossing for a reason. I would like to continue and see where this goes. I'm not asking for forever. I'm not even asking for a romantic relationship. I just want to be your friend. It sounds like you need a friend or two. Hardy, can I be your friend?"

"I have a friend. His name is Trevor. But I guess I could use one more." He says through a big smile.

Without even realizing, we ended up back at the fire station. We say our goodbyes and head our separate ways.

8

It is demo day, and I have Trevor over to help. We take down the warped and rotting deck. We carefully detached it from the house so we can reuse the header board as it looks to be in great condition. The radio is cranked and currently "Gone Country" by Alan Jackson is playing. It takes us most of the morning to remove the old deck. We take a break, and I head inside to grab a couple glasses of iced tea. I return outside and hand a glass to Trevor.

"Thanks."

"No, thank you for coming over to help me."

"I told you just call when you need help, and I will do what I can to help you. I am a man of my word. What's going on with you? You seem lighter and dare I say happier?

"Remember that mystery girl I have told you about? The one

with the bright emerald green eyes. Well, it turns out she is the architect designing our new fire station. I have run into her a couple of times. We have had several conversations and she feels the same magnetic pull I do."

"I'll be…. Hardy Morrison hit with the love bug. I thought I would never see the day again." Trevor whistles out.

"WHOA…HOLD ON. No one said anything about love. We are strictly friends. I cannot go down that road again." I retort with a gritty edge to my tone.

"I'm sorry Hardy. I didn't mean to ruin your good mood. Just do me a favor will you?"

"Yeah, anything."

"I'm serious. Please don't shut and weld the door closed on this. Friends with her is good. Just let whatever happens evolve. You deserve happiness. Don't get in your own way."

"Trevor, I can't promise that."

"Hardy, yes you can. I'm not saying profess your undying love for her. If it remains strictly platonic friendship, so be it, but don't actively sabotage it from potentially becoming more just because you're scared. You have made so much progress. I am here to support you. You are a brother to me."

All I can do is nod my head. I have tears flowing down my cheek and my throat is too tight to speak. I know he is right. But that fear is still paralyzing.

"Alright, enough of the pity party. Let's take a look at the support posts and footings. If they are still in great shape, then we can start building the new deck." Trevor says while patting me on the back.

We examine the support posts and footings. They look like they are in good shape. We decide we can still use them. Next, we review the sketch that I have for the new deck and survey the area and talk about if we have enough support posts and footings for what I want to build. After some back and forth discussion we decide the current footings are enough and in the correct spots.

We break for lunch. Lunch is a couple of sandwiches, pickles, kettle chips, and iced tea. We eat quickly, as we want to get back to work. While we eat, we discuss how we are going to attach the beams and joists. It takes us the rest of the afternoon to attach the beams and joists. We work in tandem while the radio plays our favorites 90s country tunes.

We decide to start the decking and railings tomorrow. Feeling accomplished with the progress made so far, we agree to meet at the Silver Spur for dinner and to watch the baseball game. Trevor heads home to clean up as I head inside to do the same.

The parking lot is three quarters full when I arrive. I park and head inside to the hostess stand. I look around and do not see Trevor yet.

"Hi, welcome to the Silver Spur. How many?" the hostess asks with a smile.

"Two please, with a view of the baseball game if possible. Thank you."

"Sounds good. Follow me."

I follow the hostess to a high-top table that seats four. It has a perfect view of the tv showing the pregame show. I look around the room and don't see anyone I recognize. Not unusual but sometimes I run into people I know. Yeah, sure, you know you were hoping to see Dylan. Just admit it. Whoa, where did that thought come from.

"Hi, I'm Sarah. I'll be your server tonight. Do you want to wait for the other person to arrive, or can I get you something to drink?"

The voice startles me out of my own head. "I'll take an iced tea please."

"One iced tea on the way." Sarah says

Sarah walks away and I look around and see Trevor walking in. I give him a wave, and he heads over. He sits down and remarks about how busy it is for a Thursday night. I'm glad it's busy. This is a great bar with great food and live music. I want them to be successful.

"Here is your iced tea. What can I get you to drink?" Sarah says as she sets my tea down and looks at Trevor.

I'll take a Guinness please" Trevor replies with a smile.

"One Guiness on the way." and she turns and walks to the bar.

"Great table to watch the game. Nice snag Hardy. Need the menu?" Trevor looks at me with a mocking grin.

"Nope, I know what I am getting. How about you?" I tease back

"I'm getting my usual." He says with a laugh.

Sarah returns and takes our food order. For me it is the mushroom swiss burger with steak fries. I also add an appetizer of fried mushrooms. Trevor gets the rodeo burger with steak fries and adds an appetizer of chips and salsa. We watch the first inning while we wait for our food.

Dylan stares intently at the computer screen as she takes in every last detail. The first draft of the new fire station design is complete. Now, she is reviewing it for errors before she sends it to the city for their review/comments/requested changes. This project was a challenge, yet it was fun and invigorated her. The mix of occupancy classifications within a fire station is amazing. There is office space, kitchen areas, lounge rooms, garage space, storage, mechanical, dorm rooms, shower rooms, and training area, just to name a few. Then add in the financial piece of a municipal building. Public entities are more accountable to how they spend their money than private entities. This means that designing a building that is functional to fit a variety of needs and be within a strict budget, required the use of all her skills and knowledge.

Satisfied that her first draft is ready, she sends it to her boss for review. If he approves, he will send it to the city. She leans back in her chair and lets out a huge breath that she did not realize she was holding. This calls for a little celebration. She isn't thinking of anything big, but she decides she will treat herself to dinner out for a job well done. And she knows just the place. It is a Thursday night. It shouldn't be too busy.

Her mind made up, she checks her email one last time, then powers down her computer. She grabs her purse, shuts her office door and heads to her car.

Dylan pulls into the lot and finds it full. It is busier than she expected. If anything, she will sit at the bar. There is always space at the bar. She circles the lot and finds it completely full. She snags one of the last parking spots on the side of the street. She heads inside and walks up to the hostess stand. She looks around as she waits for the hostess to return. The place is packed. All the bar seats are occupied as well. She decides to check with the hostess and see how long the waiting list is.

She had her heart set on this place and doesn't want to go anywhere else. Denise, the hostess informs her the wait is about 30 minutes. Dylan puts her name on the list and heads for the ladies room. Not paying attention as she leaves the ladies room, she bumps into someone leaving the men's room.

"I'm sorry, I wasn't paying attention. Excuse me." She says with embarrassment in her voice.

"Dylan? All is forgiven. Are you ok, you seem distracted." A familiar voice responds. She looks up and sees Hardy. Her face instantly blushes and she gets goosebumps.

"Yeah, I'm fine. I just wasn't paying attention. I'm waiting on a table to open up. It is really busy here tonight."

"Youi by yourself or with others tonight?"

"By myself. Why do you ask?

"Trevor and I have a high top that seats four. Would you like to join us?"

"I don't want to impose on a boy's night out."

"It isn't a boy's night out. Seriously, join us. That way you don't have to wait."

"Ok, if you insist. I just need to take my name off the list."

Dylan and Hardy head to the hostess stand and remove her from the list.  Hardy then leads Dylan over to the table.

"Hey man, I thought you lost your way or some…" Trevor begins to say when he notices the gorgeous lady standing next to Hardy. "I see what took you so long." He gives Hardy a wink.

"Trevor, this is Dylan. Dylan, this is Trevor.  Dylan is designing the new fire station." Hardy says as a way of introduction.

"Dude, this is the one you have been talking about!? Your description of her does not do her justice.  She is gorgeous." Trevor says as he winks at Dylan. If Hardy's face turned any deeper shade of red, he would be reclassified as a tomato.

"What did I miss in the game Trevor?" Hardy says as a way to change the conversation.

"The Rangers scored three and are now up by four." Trevor says, staring at the TV.

The waitress comes back and takes Dylan's order.  She orders a Mushroom swiss burger, steak fries, fried mushrooms and an iced tea. Hardy stares at her with his mouth partially open.

"What? I'm hungry." Dylan says while laughing.

"No, it isn't that.  We ordered the same breakfast at the cafe a few weeks ago and that is exactly what I ordered tonight.  It is weird." Hardy says trying to understand what is going on.

"Soulmates" Trevor pipes up without turning his vision from the TV.  "So Hardy, what time do we want to start again tomorrow?"

"I was thinking about 9am.  Does that work for you?"

"Yep, that works for me. Dylan should come as well if she is free. We could use an extra set of hands." Trevor says as a way to poke the bear.

"Come for what?" Dylan asks.

"We are rebuilding Hardy's deck. We have the decking, railings, and stairs left."

"If you want help, I'd love to." Dylan says.

"If you're busy, you don't have to…" Hardy starts to say.

"We would love it if you could come help." Trevor interrupts Hardy.

"Alright, I'll come help if Hardy wants me to. Do you want me to help Hardy?

"Yes, here is my address." He writes it down on a napkin and hands it to Dylan.

The rest of the evening is mostly uneventful. Trevor, Hardy, and Dylan have a great conversation while finishing their meal and watching the baseball game. Dylan finds out that Trevor is a paramedic with Lime County EMS and has been friends with Hardy for a very long time. She takes comfort in knowing that because they are such good friends, he wouldn't push for her to help them if he didn't think it was a good idea. She thinks to herself, she may have an ally in Trevor to help Hardy with whatever he needs. Hardy and Trevor both find out that Dylan grew up on a ranch in Montana and isn't as much as a city girl as she currently presents herself. She sees the big smile on Trevor's face at that revelation and takes that as a good sign.

At the end of the meal, Hardy insists on paying the tab as payment both past and future for helping with rebuilding the deck. With the tab settled, they all head out to their vehicles and head home for the night.

I wake up to the sun shining in my windows and the birds chirping. I look at the clock and it is 7am. I get out of bed and go to the kitchen to start a pot of coffee. I shower, get dressed, make my bed and walk back to the kitchen for my first cup of my daily wake me up. The first morning sip is always the best. The warmth of the cup, the aroma wafting up to my nose, and the warming bitterness as it slides down my throat and into my stomach warming me up from the inside. I take a deep breath and open the newspaper. I pair that with a light breakfast of cottage cheese and peaches.

I hear the front door open, and I look up to see Trevor walk in carrying a box from the local bakery. So much for a healthy breakfast.

"Good morning, Hardy. I knew you would be up and ready to go. I brought carbs. Load up, because we are going to burn it off today. No guilt with these today." He sets the box down on my kitchen table and opens it up.

I take a look and see a few apple fritters, fried croissants, and buttercream frosting filled long johns. Feeling my willpower dissolve on the spot, I grab an apple fritter.

"You are horrible for getting these." I practically moan as I take a bite. "I'm trying to eat healthy, and you are not helping. Thank you. These are amazing."

"Yep, we can afford a cheat day with the calories we will be burning today." He says as he grabs a filled long john.

"So why did you insist on Dylan joining us? I'm sure she is busy with work."

"Hardy, she is totally into you. Anyone can see that but you. Plus, I have a really good feeling about her. Besides, she jumped at the opportunity to help. There was no wavering with her. If there is no romantic spark between you two, which I doubt very much, I think she could be a very good friend to help keep you on track."

"I'm not looking for romance."

"Remember what I said. If it comes knocking, don't push it away. See where it takes you." Trevor reminds me of our previous conversation on the boat. Just then the doorbell rings.

"Well Trevor, that wasn't a knock." I say as we both laugh

I go to the door and open it. What I see takes my breath away. I see emerald green eyes staring at me from under a Colorado Rockies baseball cap. Her hair is in a simple ponytail. She has a red checkered flannel shirt, jeans that show her amazing figure, and western boots that show wear and tear of real work. I lose my ability to speak for a moment. Luckily Trevor is right behind me.

"Hi Dyan, come on in. We have donuts and coffee to get us started." Trevor says. I snap out of my daze.

"Yeah, come on in and get some breakfast before we start." I say, sounding like a parrot.

We eat breakfast, drink our coffee and bring out big mugs to fuel us through the morning. With our plan in place, we get started measuring, cutting, and securing the deck boards. I am impressed with Dylan. She sure knows her way around power tools and construction. She was a definite help and we were moving along at a much faster pace than just Trevor and I. We had the deck boards placed and half the railing up when we decided to break for lunch.

I grill several chicken breasts and then dice them up and make a huge batch of chicken Caesar salad, along with a large pitcher of sweet tea. We need to replace the sugar burned throughout the morning. Since it is such a nice day, we decide to eat outside on the patio.

"Thank you for inviting me, Hardy and Trevor. It feels so good to get my hands dirty and actually build something again rather than just design it. It reminds me of being back home and helping my dad on the ranch." Dylan says with a faraway look like she is remembering good times.

"You're welcome. You have helped us make so much progress and it looks so good. Not only are you a talented architect, but you are great at construction. Thank you for coming to help." I say starting to ramble on and stop myself. Trevor looks at me and gives me a knowing smile. I kick his shin under the table in warning.

"Dylan, you are a woman of many talents. I hope to see you around more." Trevor says. I give him another kick under the table. His grin just grows even wider.

With lunch finished, we all work together to clean up the dishes and head back to work. We bring a radio out and turn it on. The first song that plays is "My Town" by Montgomery Gentry.

"Oh, I love this song! It reminds me of home!" Dylan says as she begins singing along.

For the next three hours we finish the railing and the stairs. We all stand back and high five on a job well done as we look at what we built together. We clean up our mess and tools and say our goodbyes.

9

On the drive over to Sheila's I give myself a pep talk. What seemed like a good idea at the time now has me second guessing my agreement. I am meeting Sheila and Capt. Domingo for a joint session. I know deep down this is a good way to move forward, however, the fact that I am going to discuss this painful topic with my current supervisor is not lost on me.

I turn into the driveway and wind my way down to her office. I pull up next to a 20-year-old two door small pickup that has so much rust, you would confuse it to be rust colored. That isn't the car I see Capt. Domingo drive to the station. I decide to sit in my car for a few minutes thinking it is the person who has an appointment before us.
I am lost in thought listening to music when a tap on my window startles me.

"Are you going to sit out here all day or are you coming in to join us?" Sheila says as I roll my window down.

"I was waiting for the previous appointment to finish before I walked in." I say pointing to the rusty truck.

"There is no appointment before you. We are ready." Sheila says with a smile.

I nod, roll up my window and step out of my truck. Sheila and I walk into the office. I turn the corner and stop in my tracks. If it wasn't for the piercing gaze I never would have recognized Capt. Domingo. I have only ever been around him when he is in uniform. Here he sits in dusty worn western boots, dust covered jeans, an old, checkered flannel shirt, and a dusty beat up western hat sitting on his knee. He looks like a rugged cowboy. I never would have guessed.

"Sorry for the mess, I was fixing my pasture fence and lost track of time. At least I'm not the last one here." He says with a laugh. "What's wrong Morrison, cat got your tongue?"

"No, I've just never been around you outside of work. I almost didn't recognize you." I say finally able to string words together.

"So, gentleman, this is a unique circumstance. You both were involved in the same critical incident, with different experiences and now you are working together responding to very similar circumstances. How is that going?" Sheila says as an ice breaker.

"Well, I feel like the odd man out because I just found out a week ago. You both have known for a lot longer. It was a shock. But I think what was most shocking was how much it affected Capt. Domingo. For the longest time, I thought no one could understand the pain and grief I was going through.  I really understood how much the fire affected those that were there.  I was so caught up in my own grief I didn't think about anyone else that was there."

"No one is blaming you for that Hardy.  You lost your entire family in a moment.  You weren't given time to say goodbye.  That is what affected me the most.  I was able to say goodbye to my Rosalie. You did not get to say goodbye to your wife and kids.  Seeing your pain was too much for me to hold in. "Capt. Domingo says while looking directly at me.

"Yeah, but you continued on working.  I went off the deep end and let the grief consume me with self-destructive behavior. I honestly didn't care if I lived another day.  As I look back on that time, I am embarrassed by my actions." I reply back

"One would say that you have PTSD Hardy and Capt. Domingo has a moral injury." Interjects Sheila.

"Do you know I almost quit at the end of that shift?  I had my resignation letter written and called the deputy chief to meet.  I was going to resign that morning.  He convinced me to hold onto the letter and meet with Sheila first. If it wasn't for the Deputy Chief and Sheila here, I don't know what I would be doing now or if I would even be alive."

I stared at Capt. Domingo with a newfound respect for the man. He is a fighter, and I vowed to learn as much from him as I could.

"Hardy, I can see you thinking.  What are you thinking about?" This came from Sheila who has been rather quiet and just listening to us talk.

"I was thinking there is a lot I didn't know about Capt. Domingo, and I think we were meant to cross paths. I want to learn how to be more resilient. There is a lot to learn from him."

"I agree, I think fate has you two crossing paths for a reason. I think you two have a lot to offer each other. You share a bond over tragedy and can offer encouragement when one is down. You are also in a position to help others together." Sheila beams like a proud mother.

We conclude our session and go our separate ways. I shake my head as I see Captain Domingo climb in his rusty truck drive away bumping down the road. He is completely different outside of work. I decide on my way home to go for a hike. I pick up my phone and make a call. I would like some company which is a foreign feeling to me.

"Hello Hardy! How are you?" Dylan says as she answers her phone.

"Are you busy? I am thinking of hiking the trails in the state park and was wondering if you would like to join me. Hardy replies, catching Dylan by surprise.

"Yeah, I would love to join you. Where should we meet and when?"

"Meet at the trailhead parking lot in about an hour? Will that work for you?"

"I can be there in an hour. Thank you for the invite. I will see you soon."

Her dad always taught her to be prepared even if you are familiar with the area. Dylan goes through her day hike bag. She makes sure she has her knife, matches, a cup, rain jacket, extra socks, compass, whistle, several protein bars, sunscreen, bug spray, and an extra hat. She fills her large water bottle and starts heading for the trailhead parking lot.

Dylan arrives and parks her car. She does not see Hardy yet. She gathers her bag and walks over to the map looking at the different trail options. It has been a very long time since she has hiked, and she is looking forward to it. She was busy with school and establishing herself at work. She looks at her watch and estimates how much daylight is left. While she would like to do the 10-mile hike it would be cutting it close to finish before dark. That leaves the five- or seven-mile loop. She will see what Hardy has in mind.

"So which trail have you decided on?" She hears Hardy say as he approaches.

"I don't think we have enough daylight for the 10-mile loop. So that leaves the five- or seven-mile loop. I think we should do the 7-mile loop, how about you?"

"You read my mind. I agree, let's walk the seven-mile loop."

Dylan and Hardy start walking down the trail. They walk for a while in silence. It is a comfortable silence that just feels right. She takes a moment to enjoy the warm sun on her skin, the slight breeze in the air with the smell of pine wafting by. She can hear birds chattering away as she steals a glance at Hardy and notices him watching her.

"What? Do I have something on my face?" Dylan says as she discreetly wipes her face.

"No, you just look at peace and content. I wanted to soak it in." Hardy says. So, you have come well prepared for not only the hike but if we end up getting stranded. I am pleasantly surprised, where did you learn that?"

"Well, I grew up on a very large cattle ranch in Montana. It has been in my family for generations. There are times when we are out tending the cattle or moving them to other pastures that we need to spend the night out under the stars. Or something unexpected occurs and we can't make it back. When I turned 10 my father would let me join in on some of the cattle drives. He taught me what I should prepare for and that I should always be prepared for anything when out in the backcountry. He had hoped us kids would take over the ranch when the time was right."

"But you don't want to correct. Your passion is design and architecture?"

"Yes, that is my passion. The thing is there are strings attached to taking over the ranch. My mom wants me married with kids. It's not that I am against it, I just haven't met that one person that has caught my attention." Dylan replies Until now she thinks to herself. She could see a future with Hardy.

"Those are some pretty big strings. What about your siblings? Are they interested in taking over?"

"I have two older brothers. One is on the professional rodeo circuit, and the other is a smokejumper for the U.S. Forest Service based out of Idaho. Neither of them are ready to settle down, raise a family and tend to a cattle ranch."

"Ahh, so you're the baby of the family. The last one to fly from the nest. I can see why your mom is the way she is." Hardy says as he bumps his shoulder into hers and smiles.

"How about you? Parents, siblings, kids?" Dylan asks and she sees Hardy visibly wince. Uh oh, I struck a nerve on that last one. Well, he will tell me if he wants to, I guess she thinks to herself.

"My parents have passed away. It was about 10 years ago. They were both elderly and my dad probably shouldn't have been driving anymore. He pulled out in front of a semi-truck during a rainstorm and was t-boned. They both died instantly. He was completely at fault; there was nothing the truck driver could do. I have an older sister who is 20 years older than me. We rarely talk. The last I heard, she was a managing partner at some law firm in Austin Texas. I was a miracle surprise baby and even though I have a sister, I felt like an only child growing up.

I told you before I have a past. I was married with two kids. They died about 5 years ago. It is painful to talk about. I would rather talk about something else and not ruin this hike. I can't believe I even told you that much. I haven't talked about them to anyone other than my therapist or those involved. I'm still working through the pain." He gives Dylan a half smile

"I'm so sorry, Hardy. I had no idea. If you ever want to talk, I would love to hear about them. If they were your family they must have been wonderful, just like you."

Both Dylan and Hardy walk along the trail in silence digesting the heaviness of the conversation and what it means. Dylan feels like their connection is growing stronger, which gives her hope. Hardy also feels the connection growing stronger, however, that is creating anxiety and confusion.

The rest of the hike they talk about their love of the outdoors and all the activities such as fishing, camping, hiking, and hunting they use to decompress from the expectations put on them, both internally and externally. They arrive back at the trailhead and neither seem ready to leave the other. Dylan decides to go for it and gives Hardy a Hug.

"You're a good man, Hardy Morrison. Don't you forget that." She says as she gives him a squeeze then turns around and gets in her car to drive away.

I stand there staring at her car like a lost child as she drives away. Did that really happen? I ask myself. I have had these walls up for five years and I thought I had them fortified. Then enters Dylan and she has systematically and strategically started weakening them. If there was ever a person I might, and I mean might, let close to me, it would be her. The problem is, she is such a pure and good soul, I would just taint her. I can't let that happen. She deserves so much better than me. Now I am feeling guilty for entertaining the idea because it feels disrespectful to Mary, Wilma and Theo.

With my brain in overdrive, I make my way back home. I shower, make a quick sandwich and then curl up in bed with my latest spy novel while trying to ignore these competing feelings and how my bed suddenly feels empty. Woah, where did that thought come from Hardy. I think you're jumping the gun a little bit here. My conscious screams at me.

I focus back on my book. The spy infiltrates an island that is home base for a criminal enterprise as he gathers evidence to bring back to his boss. This spy is always getting himself into sticky situations and barely makes it out with his life. I have thoroughly enjoyed this book series and will be sad when it comes to an end.

"It's all your fault!" the piercing scream startles me. All I see is dense fog around me.

"I'm Sorry. I should have been there!" I yell back into the void

"We were calling out for you. Wilma and Theo were crying for their daddy!"

"I'm sorry!"

"You are forgetting about us. Our memories are fading."

"I will never forget you. I love all of you very much. I miss you Mary, and the kids."

"You are replacing us."

I wake up with a start with sweat running down my face. I look around as my eyes focus on my bedroom. My bedside lamp is still on, and my book is on my lap. I must have fallen asleep while reading. I shiver as the cold sweat cools my skin with the breeze blowing by through the open window. I look at the clock. It is 4:04am.

I get out of bed and start stripping the bedding to wash the remnants of yet another nightmare away. With my bedding in the wash, I jump in the shower to rid myself of the sweat and tension. I decide to go for a run. I have one more day before I am back on shift. I need to release this pent-up energy.

Dressed, I walk out the front door and start on a long run. I put my earbuds in and turn on my favorite music. I start running at a comfortable nine-minute a-mile pace and get settled into the rhythm as

I let my mind start to organize and categorize all these thoughts swirling in my head.

Before I realize it, the Structural Designs building is coming into view. I look over and see Dylan in her office, a soft yellow desk lamp highlighting her face as she studies something on her desk. I almost stop to get her attention, but think better of it. I don't trust myself to not break down on her and tell her about everything that is happening: the nightmares, the guilt, my conflicted feelings.

I pick up the pace before I can change my mind. I make my way to the river trail and decide to follow the river for a way. After a while, my mind is calming down and my muscles are sore, so I loop around and head towards home.

I arrive back home and see it is 7am. I ran for two and a half hours covering 15 miles. That was definitely a long run. I clearly needed it. I start my coffee pot, put the bedding into the dryer and jump back in the shower.

The rest of the day is spent staining my new deck. I have the radio on and get lost in the monotony of swiping the brush back and forth and watching the stain soak into the wood. The various wood grains     pop     out     and     highlight     the     stain.

10

I arrive at the station feeling off for some reason. I can't put my finger on it, but an uneasiness has settled in the back of my mind. I change into my uniform and help Joey with checking our equipment. Everything works as it should. We go to the kitchen to join the rest of the crew for morning roll call and a cup of coffee. We have hose line management training this morning at the training center. Then, this afternoon we are giving a fire safety talk and fire truck tour to a group of first graders at the elementary school. Looks like we have a full day ahead of us. Joey and I start the daily cleaning. We must be doing something right because Capt. Domingo and Darryl assist us with the cleaning today. Or, maybe it is because we have a full day on our plate. Maybe that is why I feel uneasy, because we have a lot to do.

We arrive at the training center and are joined by engine 1, engine

3, and ladder 2. We are using the "B" building. This is the building that is a two-story house with an attached garage. We complete sets and reps where the engine companies stretch attack lines for fire control, and the ladder company completes search and rescue. The engine companies rotate between primary, secondary, and back up lines. The ladder company alternates between search and rescue and roof operations.

We spend the two hours practicing and refining our deployment. We learn from each other's mistakes and work to tighten the deployment up. We try different ideas to make deployment more efficient and quicker in an effort to get water on fire as soon as possible. The mindset we have is the quicker we resolve the problem (put the fire out) the more tenable the space is for anyone that needs rescue.

Feeling a sense of accomplishment, we head back to the station for a shower, change of clothes and lunch. Before we can finish lunch, BEEP, BEEP, BEEP. Engine 2 995 Linda St N diabetic.

We arrive on scene ahead of Lime County EMS. We find a 65-year-old female who is confused and slurring her words. The husband says his wife is diabetic and hasn't been feeling well. She has continued to take her medication but has been unable to eat or keep anything down. We check her blood sugar and find that it is 35 dl/ml. We start an IV and administer fluids along with D10. That is a ten percent dextrose solution to help elevate blood sugar levels. Her other vital signs are within normal limits.

The patient starts to become more alert. We are able to complete a stroke assessment. The stroke assessment is negative. We are fairly certain this is a diabetic emergency. Lime County EMS arrives and

Trevor walks in with Beth right behind him. We update Trevor and Beth with what we have found out so far, our treatments, and outcomes. The patient is requesting transport to the hospital. We help the patient onto the stretcher and out to the ambulance. As the ambulance leaves, we pack up our gear and head back to the station.

With our engine restocked and report written, we finish lunch. We have a few minutes before we need to leave for the school fire safety talk. The crew sits around the table, and the discussion turns toward the ground breaking for the new fire station. The old one was demolished, and the design by Dylan was accepted at the city council meeting. The contractor will start building the new station in two weeks. The anticipated completion date is spring next year. Some of the highlights are individual dorm rooms, a larger kitchen, a workout room that is three times bigger, and a training area off the apparatus bay with movable walls, windows and a stairwell. I have to say, when I saw the design, I was impressed with Dylan's work.

We arrive at the elementary school and I grab my turnout gear and SCBA while Joey grabs some of our medical gear. We follow the school secretary to one of the first-grade classrooms. As we walk inside, we see around 60 sets of eyes watching us with barely contained excitement.

Captain Domingo starts off by introducing us. He goes on to explain that we do more than put the fire out. The kids sit as well as they can while they listen to how we help people who are stuck, have a medical problem, and also put out the fire. He tells the kids that basically if you have a problem, we are here to help. It is my turn next.

"Hi kids. I am firefighter Morrison. I have brought with me some of the clothing we wear to help keep us safe. Do you want to see it?"

"YES!" The kids yell out in unison.

"Ok, first I am going to put on my bunker pants and boots, then my nomex hood. After that I will get my jacket on and zip it all the way up. Next, is my SCBA backpack. This carries the air I will breathe in the bottle. I will now put my mask on. Listen to how my voice changes. Don't be afraid. It is still me, firefighter Morrison." I put my mask on, pull my hood to cover my head and around the mask. My voice changes to sound like a spaceperson. "Next, I will put on my helmet and lastly my gloves to keep my hands safe. Can everyone hear me?"

"Yes!" Yell out the kids.

"Does anyone have any questions?" A bunch of hands go up. I point at one kid.

"Is it hot in those clothes?"

"Yes, it can get very hot in these clothes." I point at another kid

"Why do they call your pants bunker pants?" That question stumps me. I honestly don't know. Capt. Domingo chuckles and steps in.

"It is called bunker gear because it used to be kept by the firefighters' bunks at night. Now we keep them next to the firetruck but the name has stuck." Capt. Domingo explains.

While Joey talks about the medical gear we carry and use, I start to get out of my turnout gear and set it up how I like it for efficiency. Joey talks about the cardiac monitor and all of the different vital signs that we can evaluate. He shows our first in bag with all the medications and needles. This gets the kids to yell out about how they are scared of needles. Joey talks about how we can help people and start treatment before the ambulance arrives.

After Joey finishes talking about the medical supplies. Capt. Domingo talks about fire safety. He talks about what to do if you find matches or lighters. How kids don't play with fire. He even talks about the importance of a family evacuation plan and having a meeting place to know that everyone is out of the house. He finishes with kitchen safety and not playing around the hot stove and making sure pot handles are turned in so a little hand doesn't grab a handle and tip a pot over.

The kids have been sitting as patiently as they can and it is clear they need to get up and move. We have them stand up and get in a line. We take them outside to see the fire truck. Daryl takes the lead on this and shows the kids all the tools we keep in the compartments. He shows them the hose, the irons, the New York hooks, axes, sledgehammers, bolt cutters, and a fishing net.

"Do you guys get to go fishing at work!?" some kid yells out. Daryl laughs.

"No, I wish we could though. That net is to rescue the little duckies in the spring when they fall down into the sewers."

As we are wrapping up we hear… BEEP, BEEP, BEEP. Engine 2 1586 14th ave dumpster fire next to a commercial building. Joey and I start donning our turnout gear as Capt. Domingo tells the kids to stand back from the curb and that they will get to see us drive away with our lights and sirens on. The kids start yelling with excitement and take a few steps backwards. While Capt. Domingo dons his turnout gear, Daryl makes a quick lap around the fire truck checking for open cabinet doors or hiding kids. When he ensures no one is around the truck he starts the truck, turns on the lights and sirens and exits the parking lot onto the main road.

We arrive and find a large construction dumpster fully involved with fire about 4 feet from a one-story strip mall. The fire hasn't reached the building yet. I exit out of the truck and grab the nozzle as Joey and I deploy the cross lay. Daryl gets the pump up and running and sends us water when I signal him that I am ready.

I start spraying the water on the end of the dumpster next to the building and work out from there. Once we have the majority of the fire extinguished, Joey takes the trash hook and moves items around so we can completely extinguish the fire. Daryl turns the foam on, this way we can saturate and soak the debris in foam. The foam acts as a barrier preventing the chemical reaction of fire from getting the oxygen it needs, as well as reducing the surface tension of the water and allowing it to penetrate deeper into the garbage to help extinguish the flames in the hard to reach places.

While Capt. Domingo looks for witnesses to determine if the investigation team needs to be involved, Joey and I start cleaning up the hoses and gear. We drain the water out of the hose and roll the bundles up to get the rest of the water out. We place the used bundles in an exterior compartment. We will put new hose on the engine back at the station and then wash and dry the used hose bundles.

Back at the station, I start working on the hose load while Joey, changes the SCBA bottles, washes the packs, does an after use check and then places the packs back on the engine. He then refills the old bottles with compressed air and places those bottles on the rack.

I start by unrolling the used hose and taking a bucket of mild soapy water and scrubbing the hose with a brush. I scrub the hose, rinse, then flip the hose and repeat. Once all the hose is scrubbed, we hang the hose to dry.

With our engine in working order and cleaned up, Joey and I head in to clean ourselves up for the second time for the shift. After we are clean, we start preparing dinner. On the menu tonight is grilled chicken thighs, roasted mixed vegetables, garlic and cayenne pepper infused jasmine rice. It is a simple dinner, yet it is one of the favorites with the crew. We are about halfway through the meal when we hear BEEP, BEEP, BEEP… Engine 1, Engine 2, Engine 3, Ladder 1, BC 1 respond 1740 9th Ave SW for an alarm sounding. Additional caller reporting light haze second floor.

We hurry to the apparatus and don our gear. We pulled out of the garage and turn on our lights and sirens. It looks like we will be the third arriving engine. Several possible assignments pop into my mind. We could be tasked with supplying the FDC, or we could be given the task of on deck. Engine 1 will most likely be first on scene and make their way to the second floor. Ladder one will arrive and secure utilities and most likely search the 3rd floor. Engine 3 should be next in and will most likely be tasked with primary search/ fire control first floor. That leaves FDC or on deck for us as the most likely assignment.

We arrive and stage. Command instructs us to continue staging.

It appears to be an overheated motor in the laundry room, but they are checking for any fire. We relax slightly as we listen to the updates. It is becoming rather likely we will be released from the scene shortly. Engine 2 you can return to service. With that Capt. Domingo hits the available button on the CAD and we start heading back to the station.

BEEP, BEEP, BEEP… Engine 2, Engine 4, Engine 5, Ladder, 2, Ladder 4, Squad 3 respond 718 Highland RD S Apartment fire, flames and smoke visible. Capt. Domingo turns the lights and sirens on, and we head towards highland road. Capt. Domingo reads the CAD notes and advises of possible kitchen fire, and it appears we will be first on scene.

"Morrison when we arrive start loading the skid load. I will recon quickly to determine how many loops. Whitman, grab the irons in the event we need to force entry."

"Morrison, skid load nozzle, Whitman, irons. Copy Cap." Joey and I say in unison. We arrive on scene and find Deputy Chief Delaney already on scene. The apartment building is an eight unit building with a common central area. Four units on the second floor and 4 units on the first with a staircase on one side of the common central area. Deputy Chief Delaney advises there is a kitchen fire in the second floor charlie delta unit. We start to deploy the skid load when the deputy chief stops us.

"No, residents are reporting that the occupant in the first floor alpha delta unit has not evacuated and may need help getting out. I want you guys to help him get out. I can hear the next engine coming. I will have them stretch the first line." Deputy Chief Delaney says.

The thing about the fire service is there is no arguing direct orders, especially on the fireground. We can discuss the pros and cons of decisions after the fact in the after-action review, however, in the heat of the moment, orders must be followed unless there is a safety issue being overlooked. We finish stretching the skid load to the front door, since it was already loaded on my shoulders. We then opened the door and found a light haze in the hallway. We mask up and head in. I grab the Halligan bar and place the claw end between the door and jamb. I check the door, and it is locked. I prepare myself and say "hit". Joey strikes the adze end. I ensure the tool is seated correctly and yell out "strike". Joey keeps striking the adze and while in move the tool to gain better purchase.

The next thing I know, the world goes pitch black. I yell "stop" and Joey stops. What the hell is going on? I hear Captain Domingo yell "What the hell, the fire isn't upstairs, it's right next door. The damn apartment flashed over." The heat is unbearable even in my bunkers. I pull the Halligan away from the door. The person on the other side has a better chance of survival if we keep this door closed. The next thing I know, my mouth is on fire. My mouth is the closest to the open hole in my mask where the regulator attaches. Shit! My regulator came apart from my mask. Holding my breath I try to find the regulator. I can't see anything, it is absolute pitch black. I cannot see my hands in front of my face. I tap my mask and still cannot see my hands.

I feel like I'm burning up and I can't hold my breath much longer. Where is that damn regulator? There is a really annoying and really loud alarm sounding. It sounds like the most annoying sound in the world,

and it reverberates through my head.  It is like a machine screaming the letter                    E                    without                    stopping....
EEEEEEEEEEEEEEEEEEEEEEEEEEEEEEEEEEEEEEEEEEEEEEEEEEEE.
Then it finally registers.  It's the audible horn for the fire alarm system.

Out of reflex I take a big breath in.  I can feel the searing pain go past my lips, though my mouth and down my throat.  Now I know what a steak feels like on the grill.  The pain is immediate and unrelenting.  I scream, taking another breath in.

"Captain. my regulator.  I'm breathing in fire." I mutter out through choking breaths.

"Morrison, what's wrong?" Capt. Domingo asks

"Regulator…. Out…. Hard…to…Breath" I try my best to speak. The pain intensifies with each word.  Each breath in the pain starts to lessen.  That isn't a good sign.  It means I am burning up nerve endings. The damage is still ongoing; I just can't feel it as much.

"MAYDAY, MAYDAY, MAYDAY. Firefighter down 1st floor alpha delta corner of common area.  Some sort of smoke explosion into the hallway. Need help evacuating crew." I faintly hear in the distance.

Unable to hold my breath any longer I take another breath in.  This one doesn't hurt as bad.  I cough and gag. Clean air.  I need clean air.  I drop to the floor.  I can feel the smoke all the way to the floor. There is no clean air in this room.  I am starting to feel really light headed. Get out.  I need to get out. There is no hose line.  We didn't bring one in. We were doing a simple evacuation in a hallway with light smoke.  I try searching for the door by feel. All I feel are walls. With my hands on the wall, I shuffle. Wall, shuffle, Wall, Shuffle, Wall, shuffle, Wall, shuffle,

Wall.

Oh no, I'm trapped. Panic starts to set in. This mask is suffocating me. I need to get it off NOW! I grab under the mask with my hands and lift up. OH MY GOD! The pain on my face. I can feel my face melting. With a moment of clarity I put the mask on my face and the burning intensifies. When I broke the seal of my mask on my face the rubber became very hot once exposed. Then when I put that mask back on my face, the super heated rubber literally melted to my skin. Where am I? What is going on? I feel like I am dying? I just want to go to sleep. I am no longer a firefighter, I am a simple human being trying to survive. My body feels so heavy and I feel very tired. I can't keep myself up anymore.

I feel myself lying down. I have no energy left. I just know this is the end. This is where I die. I'm coming Mary, Wilma, and Theo. I am in this black pit of suffocation and heat. I send a prayer to God.

"God, if you can hear me, I can't get out of here. I am trapped. If I am to survive this, I need your help."

An overwhelming sense of peace washes over me. Now I understand why it is believed that drowning is a peaceful way to die. I am relaxed and numb. I imagine this is what a drowning victim feels like. Don't get me wrong. There is sheer terror, pain and panic in the beginning. But now, as I lose consciousness, I feel at peace. I guess God heard me and is comforting me.

On the cusp of consciousness, I feel like I am floating. I feel my body float up and away from the floor. Then suddenly my face is ice cold. I hear what I can only describe as a loud jet engine in the background and lots of yelling. Heaven is more chaotic than I thought it would be.

I feel my body jostled around quite a bit and hear faint sirens in the background. I slowly start opening my eyes as I hear my name.

"Morrison, if you can hear me open your eyes" from a voice sounding a lot like Trevor.

"There ya go buddy! "Welcome back to the land of the living." he says and pats my shoulder.

I look around and see Joey and a police officer also in the back. They are busy removing my bunker pants and boots. Trevor places a non rebreather mask on my face and I wince at the pain.

"Sorry, but you absolutely need this. In fact, if we were live with RSI, I would be intubating you right now. Your mouth and nostrils are full of soot. We are still going through the training with medical direction." Trevor says.

RSI or Rapid Sequence Intubation is where you use chemical sedation and a paralytic to sedate the patient and then paralyze the body to place an endotracheal tube. It is used on patients who need a secure airway but still have a respiratory drive for now.

I hear Trevor give a report to the hospital.

" En route with a firefighter with 2nd degree facial burns, airway burns, soot in both oropharynx, and nasopharynx. The patient was initially unresponsive. His eyes are now open and he is starting to respond to commands. The patient is hypotensive and tachycardic. Initially oxygen saturation was 82% on room air. We have a non rebreather at 15 lpm. Oxygen sats are now 92%. Two 16 gauge IVs established. We are about five minutes out.

We arrive at the hospital and are met with a gaggle of people. I am brought to the main trauma room and attached to the blood pressure cuff, ekg electrodes, pulse ox probe, and another 1000cc bag of saline is attached to the IV line. The doc comes in and uses an endoscope and goes through my nostril and down my throat. He notes that I have soot all the way from my nasopharynx, oropharynx and down my trachea and past my vocal cords. There is concern for secondary swelling. Several doctors leave the room for a discussion.

"Hang in there Hardy. I need to finish this report, then clock off. I will return in a little bit when you get settled in a room." Trevor says while squeezing my shoulder. "Joey is going to stay with you for a while."

"Thank you but you don't need to come back." I respond.

"That's enough Morrison. You are going to need help in a little bit and another set of ears to hear what the docs have to say. You are in shock right now and will probably only hear half of what is being said. I am coming back as soon as I finish this report and clock off." He then leaves the room not giving me a chance to argue.

The nurse walks in and lets me know they are getting a room ready in the burn unit, and I will be transferred there shortly.

"Those facial burns look painful, not to mention the burns to your airway. I have pain meds here. I think you should take them."

"The pain isn't so bad right now. I'd rather not." I say.

"Once the adrenaline wears off, you are going to feel the pain. We would like to get ahead of the pain. Plus, those facial burns are going to need debridement and that is a painful process. Please let me give you the pain meds."

"Ok, I'll take them." I respond.

The ER doc walks in and gives me a long look.

"You are lucky to be alive, Hardy. I am amazed at how you are doing right now. We debated sedating you and placing an ET tube because we are concerned about secondary swelling. After some discussion with my colleagues, we have decided to hold off as you are improving with your vitals and breathing. Just so you are aware, we are still concerned about secondary swelling and your airway closing up. We are keeping the airway cart right next to your bed in the burn unit and the first sign we see of any decline, we will be sedating you and tubing you. Do you have any questions?"

"No sir, I understand. Thank you." I say with all honesty and a tear in my eye.

"Hardy, your co-worker described the situation you were in. You clearly had some divine intervention tonight. Get some rest and work on getting better." and with that he pats my shoulder and leaves the room.

The tears in my eyes start to multiply. The reality of what I just went through is starting to hit me. How am I alive? I was certain I was going to die. It had to be God. I remember praying to God, and then a feeling of overwhelming comfort and peace. Then the next thing I knew I was in the back of the ambulance. How did I get there? I will need to ask Capt. Domingo and Joey. I have a lot of questions. Also, what happened? How did the hallway go from a light haze to as black and hot as the pits of hell?

"Joey?" I ask looking at him

"Yeah, Morrison?" He replies. I can see the red rings around his eyes. It looks like he was crying.

"What happened? How did I get out?"

"I think it is best if we wait until Capt. Domingo can help explain. I don't know all the details myself. I couldn't see anything. All I know as when we got you out of the building, I thought you were dead. We all thought you were dead."

I am moved to my new room in the burn unit. I am physically and emotionally exhausted. I close my eyes.

"Hi Hardy, My name is John, and I will be your nurse for the next few hours until shift change. Let's get you settled in and let me take a look at your facial burns." John says by way of greeting. "Ok, let's get those wounds cleaned up so they can heal properly. I am going to grab my supplies and I'll be right back. This will probably be painful. Are you allergic to any pain medications?"

"No, I am not allergic to any pain meds. I don't need any, they gave me some in the ER."

"Ok, I am going to gather my supplies and I will be back."

"Knonk knock" Trevor says as he walks in with Dylan right behind him. She looks like she has been crying as well. "I'm sorry Hardy. Dylan saw it on the news and when she couldn't get a hold of you, she called me. I couldn't lie to her."

"It's ok." I say. "I'm ok." I say looking at Dylan.

"Hardy Morrison. You most certainly are not. It looks like you are still in shock. You are going to need us. We will not let you push us away by saying you are ok." Dylan replies through quiet sobs.

Nurse John comes back into the room and stops looking at everyone.

"It's ok with me if it's ok with you. They can stay." I say sweeping my arm over everyone.

"It's fine with me. Are you ready?" He looks at me.

"Yep." I say.

The first go at debriding has me literally jumping out of the bed in pain. "I think you need pain meds, Hardy. Can I give you some?" John says. I can't even speak, it hurts so much. I just nod approval. He finishes the debriding and leaves the room.

Dylan asks me how I am feeling. I answer honestly. I am confused. I am confused how I survived, and I am confused with how things went south so quickly. Just as Joey and Trevor were about to speak, Capt. Domingo walks in.

# 11

"Hardy, it is so good to see you alive." Capt. Domingo says his eyes are also red rimmed. "How are you feeling?"

"I've been better" I say through a laugh.  At least my humor is intact. Everyone laughed at that. "So, what happened?" I ask Capt. Domingo.

"Thats one question I wanted to ask you.  How did your regulator come out?

"I am not really sure.  I had the Halligan to the door frame and Joey was striking. Next thing I know is everything goes black, and it got really hot. I felt like I was on fire.  I knew we shouldn't open the door, so I told Joey to stop and I removed the Halligan from the door.  When I did that, I could feel heat funneling up through my mask and could taste smoke. It was then I realized my regulator was unhooked from my mask. I couldn't see anything. Do you think the Halligan was hooked in the regulator hose and ripped it out?

"It sure sounds like it from what you described. I heard you call out for me and say you had a problem. So, I called a mayday and then went to grab you and try to help you get the regulator connected back to the mask. But you were gone."

I dropped to the floor in search of clean air, but when I got to the floor, I realized the smoke was all the way to the floor. There was no clean air. By this time, I had taken a couple of deep breaths. I was getting disoriented and confused. I tried to find my way out, but everywhere I went, I found a wall. I couldn't find the door."

"That makes a lot of sense. I had found you at one point and tried to guide you to the door, but you pulled away from me and I had to try and find you again."

"I pulled away from you?"

"Yes, you did. I don't blame you though. By that point you were so hypoxic and I'm guessing had very high levels of carbon monoxide in your system along with all the other lethal chemicals in that smoke. I ended up on my hands and knees with Joey and we were searching for you. We found you curled up in a fetal position. You were completely dead weight and unresponsive. We thought you were dead."

"I was so tired. I just wanted to sleep. My last memory before I woke up in the back of the ambulance was praying to God. I prayed that he would hear me and that if I was to survive, I needed his help because I couldn't get myself out of there." I look up and everyone has tears in their eyes.

"God heard your prayer son and answered it. Obviously, you have more to accomplish here, and it wasn't your time to go home." Capt. Domingo stated so straight foreward that it gave me the chills.

"Joey and I were dragging you to the door when Engine 4 came through.  We were so tired we literally lifted you up and passed you up and over us to them and they just kept you up and passed you from arm to arm over them and through the door."

"So, how did that happen? How did the hallway go from good visibility to the darkest pit of hell?"

"Well, to start, the fire was not upstairs.  It was the apartment right next door.  Thank God the staircase was located where it was. It blocked most of the heat otherwise we all might have burned to death. Our best assumption is the kitchen fire grew exponentially causing a flashover of the entire unit. The pressure was so great, it bowed the main apartment door outward.  I'll have to show you a picture sometime when you're ready.  The door looks like a recurved bow.  We are very lucky the smoke did not flash on us.  It was a very dangerous situation."

"How about the person in the apartment we were starting to open up. Are they ok?"

"They weren't even home.  The apartment was empty." He says with a laugh.  "Alright, Hardy.  I have to go talk to the brass.  I wanted to check on you first and see how you were holding up.  I will stop by tomorrow and see how you are doing. Joey, your presence is also requested.  Follow me."

"I'm going to grab a cup of coffee, I'll be back in a little while."

Trevor says as he slips out before I can protest, leaving Dylan and I alone in the room.

"Hardy, when I heard about the fire on the news and then I couldn't get a hold of you, I couldn't move. I had this bad feeling in my stomach that it was you. I am so glad you are alive. I know we are friends, but I cannot lie. It feels like you mean more to me than just friends. My immediate reaction when I heard the news was heartbreaking. It felt like a piece of me was missing. I don't know how to explain it. I don't want a response from you. I just want you to listen and hear me. I don't care how long it takes, and I won't push you. Hardy, I feel like we belong together, and I think you feel it too, you are just scared. That is ok. What happened tonight is scary for me. Let's be scared together. Just think about that please."

"Ok, visiting time is over for tonight." Nurse John says as he pokes his head in the door.

"Thank you, I was just leaving." Dylan says as she kisses my forehead.

I watched her leave, and I don't know if it was the pain medications or my near death experience, but I didn't want her to go. I was so confused, one moment I was sure I was going to join my wife and kids in whatever comes after our time on earth, the next moment I am watching the woman who has systematically weakened the wall around my heart wishing she wouldn't go.

Nurse John came in for one last check before shift change. He was joined by nurse Susan.

"Alright Hardy. Try to get some rest. You have had a long day both physically and emotionally. I will see you in the morning. Nurse Susan will be here tonight in the event you need anything."

"Thank you John. I don't know how much sleep I will get, but I will try."

Both John and Susan leave the room and I am left with my thoughts. The fire plays over and over in my head. I faintly remember hearing someone screaming in the background. Sudden realization hits me. That screaming was from me. I hang my head in embarrassment. I hope no one heard that.

I don't remember falling asleep, but I must have because I wake up and it is light outside. My throat is raw and painful. I start hacking up black mucus. I blow my nose and the kleenex is full of black snot. John comes in and asks if I want breakfast. I don't think I can eat but I do ask for some juice. Maybe I can drink some calories.

John comes back and takes my vitals. He also brings in oral pain meds for me to take with my juice.

"Are you up for visitors? There is one person wishing to see you. Can I send her in?" John asks. I think that over for a little bit.

"Yes, send her in. Thank you." I say.

John goes to the door and opens it. Dylan walks in. I don't mean to judge but she looks like hell. I don't think she slept at all. I feel responsible for her feeling this way.

"How did you sleep last night Hardy?" Dylan asks

"I slept great. I feel rested." I say with a smile. I really felt like I slept great.

"That is not what Susan reported to me this morning." Adds John.

"She said you were very restless, and your heart rate and respiratory rate spiked several times over night. She said it appeared you may have been dreaming, and not good dreams."

"If I was, I don't remember. Thank God for that." I say dryly.

"The doctor will be in shortly to go over the plan with you. How is your throat feeling? Do you have any tightness, shortness of breath, or difficulty swallowing?"

"No, my throat is a little sore, and I keep coughing up black phlegm. Other than that, I can breathe just fine. My face is pretty tender though."

"Ok, I am going to complete some charting, and I will be in with the doc in a little bit."

John leaves the room, I stare at Dylan and she stares at me, tears starting to fall from her eyes. I hate that I put that sadness on her. Just one more reason why we can't be together. Now every time I go to work, she is going to wonder if it is for the last time. I feel very conflicted, again. On one hand I finally feel I am ready to let her in a little bit. Yet, on the other hand, this is what happens when I do. Tragedy strikes. A knock on the door pulls me out of my mind.

Nurse Jane walks in. She is an ER nurse and was one of my preceptors when I was in paramedic school.

"Hi Hardy. I was at roll call this morning and they were talking about a firefighter who was brought in with burn injuries. Then they said your name and I just had to come up here and see you. How are you feeling?"

"Better than yesterday."

"I can only imagine. Well, I have to get back to work. I just wanted to stop in and see how you were doing."

"Thank you Jane." Jane walks out and Hardy walks in.

"Hey Hardy, how are you feeling?" Trevor says as he walks in.

"Better than yesterday but still a little sore. I can't wait to get out of here." Before Trevor can respond the Doc walks in with John right behind him.

"Hi Mr. Morrison, I am Dr. Ernest. How are you feeling?"

"I am feeling better than yesterday. My face is still sore, but I am breathing just fine and coughing up all the soot I inhaled. When can I be released back home?"

"Well, I would like to keep you for one more night of observation. You had very high CO levels, Cyanide levels, and significant burns in your airway. While the chances of secondary swelling have reduced overnight, there is still a risk. We would like to keep you for another 24 hours just to make sure."

"Doc, I feel fine now and I only live 10 minutes away. If something happens, I can be here quickly. Please, I would really like to sleep in my own bed tonight. I think it would better help me recover."

"Do you live with anyone that can help keep an eye on you? I might entertain the idea if there is someone to watch over you."

"I can stay with him and watch him, if that is alright with Hardy." Dylan pipes up.

"I can also stay with him and help keep an eye on him." Trevor says right behind Dylan.

The doc thinks long and hard about the proposal. Finally, he relents.

"Ok, I will sign off on this plan. But you must return immediately if you feel any tightness, numbness in your mouth or throat. You must also return if you develop any shortness of breath."

"Absolutely, I will return at the first sign of trouble. Thank you very much Dr. Ernest."

"Ok, I will go chart my notes and sign off on your discharge. You are a very lucky man Mr. Morrison. Best of luck to you on your recovery, both physically and mentally."

A few hours later, all the discharge paperwork has been signed, and I am on the way to my house in Dylan's car. Trevor is following along behind us. We walk in the front door and all three of us collapse on the couches. Trevor turns a movie on and I fall asleep so fast I don't even remember what the name of the movie is. I walk up some time later to a warm body snuggling up next to me. I look over and Dylan is curled up into me with her head on my chest. She looks so peaceful, and I don't want to wake her up. I glance over and see Trevor smirking at me.

"Do you want some water?" Trevor asks. Somehow knowing what I wanted.

"Yes, please." I reply. Trevor gets up and gets me a large glass of water.

"Here you go. I also ordered dinner. It should be here in about an hour." I glance at the clock and see it is already 4pm. I slept for almost 4 hours. I must have been tired. Trevor and I watch a hunting show on TV while Dylan continues to sleep, and we wait for dinner. When dinner arrives, I gently wake Dylan up and we move to the dining room table. Trevor ordered several soups, a large caesar salad and several large jugs of iced tea. The dinner tasted great and it was tolerable to eat.

Trevor and Dylan stayed with me for the next two days until I had my follow up appointment with the burn clinic. My follow up went well. My physical wounds are healing quite nicely. Mentally, I am still a mess. I have woken myself up a couple times in the middle of reliving the fire. Each time, both Dylan and Trevor have come running into my room to make sure I am ok. I have a meeting with Capt. Domingo and the BC later today. I am no longer taking the pain meds and am able to function on my own. I thank both Dylan and Trevor but I feel I do not need a 24/7 babysitter anymore. I need some time to myself to process everything that has happened. I also need to see Sheila. She will help me work through this.

# 12

I arrive at headquarters 15 minutes before the meeting time.  I hate being late.  I sit in my truck and listen to the radio trying to steady my nerves.  I know I didn't do anything wrong but any after action review involving death or serious injury is stressful.  I laugh at the song playing. It is "Killing Time" by Clint Black.  When the song finishes, I take a deep breath and exit my truck.

I walk in the front door and wave at Gladys, the administrative assistant.  She waves back and I head to the conference room.  Capt. Domingo, Deputy Chief Delaney, and Fire Chief Foster are there as well. We are just waiting for Battalion Chief Stanford to arrive.  I don't remember Battalion Chief Stanford being there.  He was on the fire alarm just prior to the call.

Once everyone takes their seat, the after-action review commences. This is a leadership after action review. The standard after action review has already taken place with the crews involved. It was the day after the fire when I was still in the hospital.

"Thank you all for joining this after-action review of the fire on Highland Rd S resulting in a serious injury to firefighter Morrison." Chief Foster starts.

"To start, the fire was incorrectly identified as being on the second level of the structure based on witness statements. A 360 visual check of the structure was not completed prior to the arrival of the first arriving engine and subsequent assignment given. After reviewing the time stamps of the critical incident factors, it is conceivable that had the order to make a rescue not been given, the first in crew very likely would have had the line to the upstairs door apartment when the bottom unit flashed. This could have caused the entire crew to be trapped on the upper level with no egress, resulting in more injuries or possibly fatalities."

I am shocked. What I thought was a mistake by the Deputy Chief, and it was a mistake, actually may have saved not only my life but also the lives of Joey and Capt. Domingo. As hot as it was on the first floor, it would have been hotter on the second floor as heat and hot gasses rise. The temperature was most likely higher than what our turngear is rated for.

"As for the SCBA worn by firefighter Morrison, it was found structurally intact and in working order. We could not get it to fail. We will note, however, that there have been documented cases where the wearer hears the regulator click in when in fact it is only clicked in halfway, leaving it vulnerable to detach with enough force. We believe this may have been the case, either due to the pressure when the apartment flashed or potentially could have been hooked by a tool firefighter Morrison was using." This came from Deputy Chief Delaney

"We have identified several areas for additional training to include scene size up and verification of information received from citizens, proper communications, SCBA functions/use, mayday events, as well as the importance of crew integrity. Because we had excellent crew integrity we are not talking about a line of duty death here."

Several more discussions take place, and I zone out thinking about how I owe my life to Capt. Domingo. If it wasn't for him, I would surely be dead. He may be unusual and do things his own way at times, however, when the rubber meets the road, his actions are very heroic. I tune back in when I hear my name.

"Firefighter Morrison, you are relieved from shift work for the next two weeks. You will receive your full base pay. We understand physically, you have been cleared to return to work. We want to make sure mentally you are ready to return. We have a list of mental health professionals that we would like you to look at and meet with one of them to discuss the incident and coping techniques. Do you have any questions?" Chief Foster says.

"I already see a mental health professional; her name is Sheila. I would like to continue with her as I have built a good rapport with her. Also, I would like to take an additional 4 weeks of PTO before I return to work. I have a feeling I am going to need it while I figure a few things out." I hope they will agree.

"Sheila is on our list.  I would encourage you to reach out to Sheila.  As for your PTO request.  It is approved.  You will have two weeks paid by the department and 4 weeks annual leave after that. If you need help or assistance with anything.  And I mean anything, please reach out to DC Delaney, Capt. Domingo, one of your coworkers or myself. You are a valued member of our team, and we want to help you cope with the trauma you experienced."

The meeting adjourned and I caught up to Capt. Domingo.  He was headed for the parking lot.  "Hey cap, wait up." I say as I run after him.

"Hey, Morrison.  I am so glad to see you up right." He says with a laugh.

"I Just wanted to say thank you for saving my life.  If it wasn't for your actions, I am certain I would have died in there.  It would have been easy for you to bail out given the conditions, yet you stayed with me and helped get me out. I am forever in your debt." I say with tears starting to form in my eyes.

"Morrison I would never leave someone behind.  That was the worst fire condition I had ever been in. As soon as you told me your SCBA was malfunctioning I knew that we were either getting out together or dying together.  Whatever happened, it was going to happen to both of us.  I am just glad Joey, and I were able to get you to the door and the backup team was right there to take over.  Do you realize it was less than two minutes from when the fire flashed to the time you were removed from the building? It felt like forever and a day to me."

"It was less than two minutes? I didn't realize that.  It felt like an eternity to me." I say "Well, I just wanted to say thank you for saving my life. I have a few things to work through, and I think best when I am away from the hustle and bustle of the city and technology. I plan to head to the land my family owns in Montana for a while. I want to build a rustic cabin and work with my hands while my brain sorts things out. There is no cell coverage there so please don't be alarmed if you can't get a hold of me."

"Thanks for the heads up. You know how to reach me if needed. Please, if you need something, call me. I don't care what time of day or night."

"I will. Thank you, captain."

I arrive at Sheila's office and sit in my truck for a little bit listening to the radio. I am a nervous ball of energy, and my knee bounces up and down while I close my eyes and try to slow my breathing. Feeling slightly better, I shut my truck off and step out. I stand in the sunlight and close my eyes. I take in the sound of the stream flowing by the wind rustling the trees, the birds chirping, and the squirrels tromping through the forest floor. I take one more deep breath and head into the office. *Ding*

"Good morning, Hardy. Are you ready?" Sheila says with a smile as she looks up from her computer.

"As ready as ever." I smile at her. A genuine smile, not a fake smile. It actually hurts my face.

"So, I heard a little about what happened from the department. I want to hear what happened from your experience. Mind telling me what happened?"

"Well, we responded to an apartment fire and were the first engine on scene. The Deputy Chief arrived before us and advised us the residents stated there was a kitchen fire on the second floor. As we were deploying our attack line, the Deputy Chief reassigned us to help rescue a resident on the first floor that was reported to still be in his apartment. We were directed to leave the line at the front door for the next arriving crew to attack the fire. We made our way inside and the common hallway had light lazy smoke, but we could still see all the way to the other end. I had the Halligan and Joey had the axe. I checked the door and found it locked. I placed the Halligan and had Joey strike it with the axe to force the door. Before we could force the door, everything went black, and it became extremely hot. It turns out the fire was on the first floor right next to us." I pause to collect my thoughts.

"And what did that do to you?" Sheila asks

"I was really confused. At first, I didn't know the fire was right next to us until Capt. Domingo said it. At that point I knew whoever was on the other side of the door had a better chance of survival as long as we kept this door closed. So, I pulled the Halligan away and the next thing I know, my regulator is disconnected from my mask, and I am sucking in super-heated gases and smoke. It was hard to breathe, and I couldn't find my way out. I remember hearing Capt. Domingo call a mayday. I was getting really tired and drowsy. I remember dropping to the floor to find clean air. There was none. I prayed to God that I couldn't rescue myself and if I was to survive, I needed His help. I remember floating through the air and my face getting cold. I woke up in the back of the ambulance on the way to the hospital."

"Wow, that is a lot to process. How are you doing?"

"Honestly, I feel lucky to be alive. If it weren't for Capt. Domingo and Joey, I would have died. I should have died. What I am struggling with the most is after the incident when I was in the hospital. I have struck up a friendship with a woman. I think she wants more than a friendship, but I am having a hard time with that."

"When did this all start?"

"She is the architect hired to design the new fire station. I admit there is a magnetic pull between us. But she is so good and kindhearted, I don't want to bring sadness into her life. What I saw in the hospital, I don't ever want to see in her eyes again. She was scared, sad, I could literally see her heart breaking. I know because that is how I imagined I looked when I found out about my family. She has systematically and covertly broken down the wall around my heart. If there was a person I would be willing to consider, it would be her. I just don't want to be the one that extinguishes the light in her eyes, and I am afraid this job and my history will do that."

"But what if the opposite is true? She seems like a strong woman from what you have described. What if she is the one who brings that life back into your eyes? Have you thought about that?

"No, I haven't thought about that." I say. Sheila can see that I am thinking. She lets the silence linger on. I really hadn't thought about it from that angle. I have so much to think about. I need to clear my head.

I decided, first thing tomorrow I am headed to Montana to be by myself to sort out my thoughts and emotions.

"I can see you are thinking about those last questions. How about we call an end to this session. Think about what you can offer each other. We had talked earlier about accepting help. You have Trevor, but another perspective might be helpful. Plus, she isn't in public safety, she will see this from a different lens. If you're willing to listen to her." Sheila offers.

"Thank you, Sheila. As always, you have given me a lot to think about. That is one thing I like about you. You are willing to ask the hard questions." I reply.

I leave her office and get back in my truck. The song playing on the radio is "Life's a Dance" by John Michael Montgomery. I've heard this song a thousand times before but as I sit and really listen to the lyrics, I begin to understand the song. I take a slow meandering drive back home. I like to just drive around sometimes and listen to the radio. The songs wash over me, and the lyrics sink in.

After driving for an hour, I arrive back home and start gathering my supplies. I have just under six weeks. I am going to make as much progress as I can on my little cabin in the middle of nowhere. I gather all my hand tools. Saws, hammer, nails, planers of various sizes, a square, wood pencils, tool sharpeners, etc.

I check, double check, and triple check my back country backpack for all my needed supplies. I also make a list for the grocery store. I add items such as trail mix, granola, jerkies, root vegetables, as they last the longest without refrigeration, and hydration tabs to add to water. I plan on fishing and trapping for my meat, the jerky is a backup in the event I am unsuccessful in my attempts. I am skilled with fishing, hunting, and trapping but even the best strike out occasionally. It is best to be prepared.

As I gather all my equipment and put it in an organized pile, I feel a sense of calm and rightness flow through my body. I know I am making the right choice. I need this time to connect with myself and nature without the distraction of modern convenience and technology. I double-check all the supplies I have laid out and am confident I have everything I need. I then make homemade shrimp alfredo sauce to pour over linguine. It is going to be a while before I have pasta again. I clean up from dinner and wipe the kitchen down. I then vacuum all the carpets and wash the wood floors. After I make my house spotless, I curl up into bed with the latest spy novel and start to read.

# 13

The morning sunlight filters through my window and over my bed waking me up.  I yawn and stretch and hear the birds chatter outside.  I meander down to the kitchen and start a pot of coffee.  I go back to the bedroom and take a shower reveling in the feel of the warm water massaging my skin.  Bathing for the next few weeks is going to consist of a dunk in the cold river with a bar of soap.

I stay in the warm shower for an extra few minutes just letting the jets massage my back and shoulders. Toweled off and dressed, I make my way back to the kitchen and pour a cup of coffee.  I inhale deeply as I bring the cup to my mouth savoring the aroma.  I take a long deep sip and let the bitter brew sit in my mouth for a moment before I swallow it.  I'll make cowboy coffee over the campfire, but it just isn't the same as I make at home. For breakfast, I finish the rest of the fresh fruit.

I load up all my gear into my truck and take the trash bag with me on my way out. I place the trash container at the curb and pull out of my driveway.

I pull into the grocery store parking lot and grab my list.  As I am walking up and down the isles grabbing my supplies I run into Trevor.

"Hey Hardy, how are you doing?" Trevor says as he claps me on the back.

"I'm doing well so far.  I am taking some time off and heading to Montana. I'll be gone for about a month." He knows my family has land, although he doesn't know exactly where or how much.

"Sounds like soul searching time.  Are you sure you're ok?" Trevor asks tentatively

"Honestly, this is the most relaxed I have felt.  I have a few things to think about."

"Ok, I must ask.  Are you planning on harming yourself? They say that those that make the decision to end their life find peace once the decision has been made and appear happy.  Is that you?"

"Trevor, I appreciate the concern.  I truly am not contemplating it or even thinking about it.  You know me, I think better out in the middle of nature.  I do appreciate you asking the hard questions. "

"You're welcome.  I believe you.  Does some of your soul searching involve a beautiful girl with bright green eyes named Dylan?"

"Yes, that is part of it.  I'm torn.  She has been successful at taking down the walls I have put up, but I'm afraid I will only bring her heartache. I have a lot to think about.  While I am thinking, I am going to start building that little cabin I have always wanted to build."

"Ok, have fun.  You know how to get a hold of me if you need anything.  I remember you telling me before that there is no cell service on your family land."

"I will. I will call you when I am back in town."

Trevor heads off to finish his shopping and I find the rest of the items on my list and head to the registers. I pay for my items and load them into my truck. Next stop is the gas station to top off my gas tank. After I fill up, I grab an extra-large cup of coffee and a bag of cashews, and I am ready to hit the road. I hear "Guitars and Cadillacs" by Dwight Yoakam playing and I turn the radio up. I wish I could dance like him. He has such a stage presence, and I get lost in the song as I merge onto the highway heading north.

After about four and a half hours of driving with a fuel stop, I arrive at the minimum maintenance dirt road that serves as the eastern property line between the land my family owns and our neighbor. I don't know who owns the land to our East. I have never met them. It could be a rancher, a family trust, a corporation, or some celebrity. Up here in Montana, it is anyone's guess.

I park my truck by the grove of poplar trees that I always park by. This way, I always know where my vehicle is. These trees have been around for as long as I can remember. When navigating in the backcountry it is always good to have a compass, but also to look for long standing visuals to help guide you. The site I have picked out is northwest of here, therefore if I need my vehicle, it is southeast of my campsite by the grove of poplar trees. I gather my backpack, root vegetables, and a couple cast iron pots to cook in. I also grab my fishing rod and small tackle box. I leave my snares, traps and woodworking tools in my truck. That will be a job for tomorrow.

Right now, my focus is on making my shelter, starting a fire for cooking and catching my dinner. With all my stuff secured to my backpack, I set out. I have about 4 miles to the site I picked out. With the terrain and weight of my pack, I figure it will take about 2 and a half hours of hiking to get there.

I walk in a northwest direction. I check my compass, find a landmark in the distance and talk to that point. Once I get there, I check my compass to ensure I didn't wander off track. Once I have confirmed my heading, I pick out another landmark and walk there. I repeat this process over and over again. I love this tried-and-true way of navigation. People get too comfortable with electronic maps and the internet to tell them where to go. It is such a relief to be out in nature and use what nature gives us to navigate around.

I crest a small hill and see the wide-open prairie to my right, semi-dense forest to my left with the small stream coming down from the mountains through both the forest and prairie. I find an old fallen tree that is propped about 4 feet off the ground. I have used this tree in the past as the cross beam for my lean-to.

I set my pack down and finish the water in my water bottle. I walk down to the stream and take a look. It is moving slightly faster than I remember, there must be more water coming down the mountain. I dip my water bottle into the cold liquid and fill it up. I take a drink and feel the ice cold, clean and refreshing water satisfies my thirst. There is nothing like fresh mountain water. Untouched by human hands. There is nothing like this back in the city.

Feeling refreshed, I gather a bunch of six-foot length approximately one to two inches in diameter branches to lean up against the tree. These will be the back supports of my lean-to. I will fill in the gaps with leaves, moss and prairie grass. With my shelter built and ready for occupation, I work on clearing an area for my "kitchen". I clear out an area about 7 feet away from my lean-to. I pull all the grass up and get down to clean soil. Then I dig down about half a foot or so. I gather stones from the creek and line those around the edge. The firepit serves two purposes, the first is for warmth at night and the second is to cook my food.

I gather logs and split them to make firewood. Once I have a good amount prepared, I start a fire. With the fire going, I walk down to the edge of the stream and cast out my line. It is a fairly decent sized stream with plenty of fish. It doesn't take me long to catch a decent sized fish that will be enough for dinner.

I take the fish back to camp and cut the meaty filets out. I peel and quarter a potato, an onion, and a couple of carrots. I take a moment to sit and observe my surroundings while the fire burns creating good cooking coals. I watch a couple deer frolic through the prairie, completely unaware I am here. I look up at the bright blue sky with white wispy clouds floating by occasionally. The scent of pine is carried by the winds as they come down off the mountain in the distance. I take a deep breath thankful that I am a part of this. Living in the city can be hectic, even crazy at times. I love coming out here to reset my soul.

The coals are perfect for cooking. I set the cast iron pan right on top of them and let it heat up. Once the pan is ready, I place the carrots, onions and potatoes in to cook. Once the potatoes and carrots are almost finished, I add the fish. I take the cast iron off the fire and let the fish finish while the pan cools. I grab my small plate and fork and dig into my meal. It isn't anything extravagant, but it sure hits the spot and fills my belly. I add another log onto the fire to keep it going and set off for an evening hike.

I put my backpack on and make sure I have my compass, whistle (good for making noise and scaring off aggressive wildlife) and water bottle. I decide to follow the stream towards the mountains. After a few minutes of hiking, my thoughts land on Dylan. I wonder what she is doing right now. A small part of me wishes she were here with me, but right now I just need to be alone.

I hike for about an hour before I turn around and start to head back to camp. Looking at the sun angle, I have about 2 hours left of daylight. I would like to split more wood before nightfall. Arriving back at camp, I finish my water bottle and fill it up in the stream before going back to my camp. I spend the rest of the daylight splitting firewood. As dusk turns to night I walk out away from the glow of the fire and look up.

What I see is absolutely stunning. It gets me every time. There are millions of dots of lights all over the sky. On a clear night like tonight, the sky is just a big sea of stars. Getting my fill of the stars and feeling the night chill start to approach, I walk back to the fire and add a couple more logs. I then curl up in my sleeping bag that I placed in my lean-to and quickly fall asleep.

Dylan sat at her desk working on her next project. The problem is she can't focus. Hardy isn't answering his phone. She has called several times, and it goes right to voicemail. She even drove to his house yesterday and everything was closed up. It looks like no one is home. She is worried about him. He has been through a lot of trauma over the last few years and his entire life has been scrambled. Yet, she can still see the resilience showing in his eyes. He is a fighter. Well, so is she. She is going to fight for him and with him.

She turns her attention back to her computer screen and stairs at the project. It just doesn't look right, but she is unable to identify what is exactly wrong with the design. Blowing out a large breath of frustration she looks out of the window. It is a nice day in the 60s with a little cloud cover and a slight breeze. She decides to go for a run and clear her head. Maybe, just maybe her brain will figure out her design, and Hardy will return her calls.

She puts her earbuds in as she exits the building. She pulls up her play list for running and sets off at a comfortable pace. With her pace and route on auto pilot and music playing, her mind wanders to her current design. Mentally she goes over every detail trying to identify what she is missing. She turns down a street and is running by the public works building when she sees the firefighters outside in the middle of a PT session. Joey sees her and calls out to her. Looking both ways, she crosses the street and runs up to Joey. She even sees Daryl and Capt. Domingo participating.

"Hey Dylan, it's good to see you again." Joey says wiping sweat off his face with his shirt.

"Hey Joey, how is the day going for you guys?" Dylan responds while nodding at Daryl and Capt. Domingo.

"Shift has been good so far. We have a busy afternoon, so we are getting our workout in this morning."

"So I haven't been able to get a hold of Hardy.  Do any of you know where he is? He has always answered my calls, but for the last two days his phone goes straight to voicemail."

"I think I can help a little with that." Capt. Domingo says as he approaches. "Hardy told me after our meeting with the brass that he was heading to some land that his family owns in Montana. He said he wanted to build the small cabin that he has always dreamed of building. He told me not to be alarmed but there is no cell phone service where the land is. If you call Treavor, he might know more. They have been friends for a long time."

"Ok, thank you so much.  I better let you guys get back to your PT session.  Thanks again and have a safe day." Dylan says as she puts her ear buds back in and starts running.

Running down the block and turning to head back to the office, it hits her.  She knows what is wrong with the design.  The company wants to include a gym to attract employees.  They have a new wellness program that allows employees to workout and are looking to incorporate gym space in the building.  She has a gym room but what is missing is an outdoor workout space.  She has decided to include a large overhead rollup door on the exterior gym wall.  With the exterior rollup door, it can be opened to allow fresh air in or allow people to bring equipment outside.  Thank you Capt. Domingo and company.  You helped in more ways than one she thinks to herself.

Dylan arrives back at the office and after a quick shower and clothing change, she gets started on updating her design. She spends the entire afternoon lost in thought and furiously working to finish this project that the knock on her door startles her.

"Hey Dylan, I didn't realize anyone was still here. Are you doing ok? It is seven pm and you are normally not here this late" Her boss says.

"Is it really seven?" She says looking at the clock and wincing. "Yeah, I am fine. I had some inspiration for this project while I was on a run this morning and wanted to get it all in the design before I forget it. I am almost finished. I will lock up when I leave."

"Sounds good. We appreciate everything you have done here. Don't work too late tonight, ok?" He says as he turns and leaves.

Dylan spends another 30 minutes finishing up her work, sends off her final edition to her boss, then logs off the computer. Shutting her office door, she grabs her cell phone and dials a number. The other end picks up as she is locking the main door.

"Hey Dylan, is everything ok?"

"Hey yourself, are you free tonight? I have some questions that I hope you will be able to answer."

"Yeah, I am free. Meet at the Silver Spur in 30 minutes?

"That sounds perfect. I haven't had dinner yet. I will see you there" Dylan hangs up the phone and walks to her car.

Trevor sits at a high-top nursing a Guinness and watching the Rockies game. His thoughts go to the phone call he received about 20 minutes ago. He thinks he knows what it is about and hopes he has some answers to point her in the right direction. He knows she is very intelligent, and she grew up on a ranch. Maybe she will be able to track him down.

Trevor looks up and sees Dylan's piercing green eyes laser focused on him as she enters. He can see why Hardy has himself tied up in knots. Dylan is a stunner but beyond that, she is such a kind and friendly soul. She plops down on the chair across from him and lets out a haggard breath.

"Thank you for meeting with me Trevor, I really appreciate it."

"No problem. So you have some questions for me?"

"Hardy isn't answering his phone, in fact it is shut off. Do you know where he is and if he is ok?"

"Yeah, kind of. I ran into him at the grocery store a couple of mornings ago. He was getting supplies and leaving town. His family owns about 20,000 acres of land in Montana south of Butte. He needed some time away to think. The area he is in doesn't have good cell phone coverage. I asked him very directly if he was thinking of harming himself. He said no. I believe him. He does this from time to time when he needs to get away and think."

Dylan can understand that; she does the same thing. When she needs to get away, she goes back home. Then it hit her, her parents' ranch is outside of Butte as well.

"You said he needed time to think. Think about what?"

"Honestly, I believe he needs to think about you and a relationship. He said for the longest time he would never be involved in a relationship again, but I think you have that boy tied up in knots and second guessing that resolve."

Dylan could only hope that is what he is thinking about. Hardy is the first man she ever even thought about a future with. She isn't going to give up if there is hope. He has sent mixed signals but has never said he isn't interested.

"What can I get you dear?" the waitress asks as she approaches.

"I'll take a Guinness and a mushroom Swiss burger with steak fries please." Dylan hands the menu to the waitress. "Thank you."

Trevor shakes his head and laughs.

"What?"

"You two are meant for each other if I am being honest. Hardy always gets the mushroom Swiss burger with steak fries. Before his world collapsed, he would pair it with a Guiness. Now it is a sweet tea."

"I wish he would see that." Dylan says with an exasperated sigh

"He will, eventually. Did he tell you about his history?"

"Not the details. Only that he had a wife and kids, but they died."

"I won't tell you the rest. That is his story to tell when he is ready. But I will say, it completely wrecked him. Just be patient if you can. If you can't, then you need to walk away. I don't want you to walk away. I can see you two are meant for each other and I think you can help him tremendously."

"I'm not going anywhere unless Hardy tells me he isn't interested. I think I am in love with him."

Trevor smiles. "Well then, welcome to the family. I love him like a brother."

"My family ranch is outside of Butte. Do you think I should go find him? I know the area and wilderness survival. Do you think he would be happy to see me if I could locate him?"

"I think he would be shocked, but once the shock wore off, pleasantly surprised."

"I'm going to do it. I have the time to take off work. I will start looking at plat maps and county property information tomorrow."

"Good for you Dylan. Go get him. If you need help just let me know."

Trevor and Dylan finish their meal and watch the rest of the Rockies game. They make idle chit chat and other small conversations to get to know each other a little better. If everything goes well, they will be seeing a lot of each other and be allies in helping Hardy on his journey to manage his PTSD symptoms.

At the conclusion of the game, they split the bill and head out into the parking lot. Trevor wishes her good luck and asks her to take good care of him when she finds him.

Dylan climbs in her car and heads home for bed. She has a busy day tomorrow and she is going to need to be well rested.

# 14

I have spent the last couple of days hauling my tools from my truck to the camp site and starting on the floor of the cabin. I made a small sled with logs, branches, and braided prairie grass as a pull rope. It helped speed the process up as I was able to bring his tools to camp in two trips. What I am building is a small trapper's cabin. It is a small 15 feet by 15 feet cabin.

I have about a dozen 15-foot-long logs with the branches trimmed off. I figure I need about two dozen more for the walls. I am pretty tired and need a break from cutting down trees and trimming branches. I decided to start notching and stacking the logs I currently have. Seeing the walls go up gives me extra motivation to continue. This part is mentally easy but physically demanding. It gives my mind time to wander.

I think about Dylan and what she is currently doing. She has probably tried to call me. I wanted to call her and let her know what I was doing, but I chickened out. I miss her laugh and her smile. I wonder if she is thinking about me. I wouldn't be surprised if she called Trevor. I fit two logs together and pound them into the ground to form a solid base. I take out some of my frustration on the logs.

*Pound* "Why" *pound* "am" *pound* "I" *pound* "like" *pound* "this" *pound*

Feeling a little better after my vent session, I continue on placing the other two logs. I have them buried into the ground about halfway. This way critters will have to dig under to get inside. Next, I measure and mark the area I need to notch out on the second layer of logs. I smile as I remember building with my Lincoln Log set as a kid. This is the adult version.

It takes me the next two days to finish placing all 12 logs that I had prepared. I have been eating fish and vegetables for the last few days and while I love fish, I need to change the menu. I take a morning to set out and find good locations to set my snares. My hope is to snare a hare. I laugh at my own little joke.

I only set out three snares. My fear is capturing more than one hare. That would be wasteful considering I am the only one here and I don't have a way of preserving the meat. My stomach rumbles as I think of a small pot of bubbling hare soup. With my snares set, I go back to finding and cutting down trees. I cut and trim trees in groups of four. This breaks up the monotony of the tasks and lets me work different muscles while giving others a break. I can work more efficiently this way.

I am cutting branches and trimming the length of the logs to have each be exactly 15 feet in length when I hear a squeal coming from the direction of a snare. I drop my tools except for the small hatchet and head toward the sound. When I arrive, I find a decent-sized hare with its leg caught in the snare. I don't like needless suffering; I quickly kill the hare. I value life, I'm not a monster, but I also need to eat. I say a prayer of thanks to God for providing me with this meat. I pack up the snare and go to the other two snares and also pack them up.

Back at camp I take a break from cabin building to skin and clean the hare. I cut the meat off the bones and wash the meat off in the stream. I remove all the organs and entrails and then fill a small cast iron pot with water. I place the pot on the fire and place the hare carcass in the pot of water. This will help flavor the soup. I let the carcass boil in the water for a few hours while I go back to building my cabin.

I get another level completed on the cabin walls. Right now, it is four feet high. I am halfway there. It will be an 8-foot-tall trapper cabin. I figure this is a good stopping point for today. I take out a knife and I start cutting up a couple of carrots, a potato, and an onion. Once those are cut into pieces, I pull the carcass out of the boiling water and add the hare meat and veggies. While the soup cooks, I stroll down to the stream edge to wash my knife and makeshift cutting board that I made from scrap wood and refill my water bottle.

I also decide to bathe. I strip down and walk into the water with my bar of soap. The water is cool and initially takes my breath away. I recover quickly and dunk my body under water. I then lather up and rinse off. I then use the sun to dry off as I walk back to camp. I am not worried about anyone seeing me as there is no one around for miles.

As I approach my camp, I can smell the soup, and my stomach rumbles its agreement. Now dried off, I put my clothes on and ladle soup into my coffee/soup cup. I savor the broth as I take a sip. Hare can be pretty gamey in taste. It does take some getting used to but compared to my steady diet of fish, it is a nice change of menu. I consume 2 more bowls of the soup, and it is all gone. My stomach is pleasantly full. I clean my cookware and head off for an evening walk.

During my walk, I think about everything that has happened since the night of the fire. The good, the bad, and the ugly. The ugly was not recognizing the hold PTSD had on me and allowing my life to spiral out of control. The bad is the constant nightmares and keeping myself closed off. The good is how persistent Trevor has been to help me through everything, even when I pushed him away. Another good thing has been Dylan and how she has systematically taken down the walls I have put up. I really want to explore this chemistry with Dylan, but to be honest, I'm frightened. I don't want to experience the pain of heartbreak again. I think about the work fire and my brush with death and think about what it means. I have heard it said by multiple people that it looks like divine intervention. I should have died, yet I firmly believe I was saved by God. I think about the meaning of that and why I am still here.

As the sun starts to set, I arrived back at camp and I put a couple more logs on the fire and crawl into my sleeping bag. I look at the stars as I fall asleep wondering if they are looking down towards me.

Dylan has been searching online records for the last several days. She cannot find any land owned by anyone with the last name Morrison in the area of Butte. She puts her head in her hands and leans on the desk to think. Then it hits her, some of the more rural counties have not made the migration to the digital age. She decides to make a trip home. She calls her boss and takes a couple weeks of vacation.

With her vacation approved, she starts packing. She packs her clothes in a suitcase. That was the easy part. She stares at her back country bag. If she is serious about going out and finding him, she needs to bring it with her. She double checks her bag and ensures that she has everything she needs. Dylan calls her mother to let her know she is coming for another visit.

With everything ready to head out in the morning, she sits down to read her latest romance novel. She spends 20 minutes reading and re-reading one page. Her nerves are getting the better of her. She blows out a frustrated sigh and grabs her earbuds. She changes quickly and puts on her running shoes and pulls her hair back into a high ponytail.

As she is running, she can hear the steady rhythm of her feet hitting the road. It is late evening, and the streets are mostly empty. Her mind starts to wander to Hardy and how he is doing. It has been less than a year since they have met, but there is something about him that just pulls her in. She admits he is very good looking, but it goes way beyond that. On the exterior he projects a closed off feeling that tries to keep people away.  She sees through it.  Inside, he is a gentle soul with a heart of gold. That is what she finds most attractive and why she is pursuing him.

Every guy she has met until this point has been a conceited individual who is looking for a stay at home chef, maid, and babysitter. Hardy is different. From their conversations, she can see that he is interested in a true partner, someone to grow with, share in pain and triumph, and someone who will challenge and encourage.  Feeling the nervousness leave her body, she heads back home.  After a quick shower, she curls up in bed to read and is asleep before she even finishes a page.

Dylan wakes up to the sunlight streaming in her bedroom window and smiles.  She replays the dream she had about Hardy and really hopes it is foreshadowing the future. She gets dressed and packs up her car. She swings by the local coffee shop and grabs a coffee and breakfast sandwich.

After filling up her gas tank, she heads onto the freeway and towards home.  She hasn't felt this excited, anxious, and unsure since she was a teenager, and it's all over a boy, no wait, it's all over a man.  She isn't a high school girl crushing over a boy anymore. She continues driving along the interstate while singing along to the songs on the radio.

Turning down the long gravel driveway, the farmhouse comes into view after cresting a small hill. Dylan looks to the left towards the horse corral and sees Daisy trotting up to the fence. Daisy gives a whine as she passes by. Pulling up to the house, her mother comes out wiping her hands on her apron.

"Dylan, welcome home!"

"Hey momma. I'm just going to bring my suitcase in, and I'll give you a hand."

Dylan brings her suitcase to her old room upstairs and then heads down to the kitchen to help her mother.

"Hey mom, what do you need help with?"

"I have a pot pie in the oven. Can you help me roll out biscuits from this dough?"

"Sure thing." Dylan washes her hands and grabs a chunk of dough.

"So, what are you doing back home again? I mean, I'm always happy to see you but this is twice in several months, when before that it was a year or more in between visits. Are you ok?"

"Yeah, I'm fine. I've come up here to find someone."

"And who might this someone be?"

"He is a friend I met in Blue River. He almost died in a fire a few weeks ago. He has taken some time off and pretty much went off the grid. His coworkers say his family owns land up here. They think he may be up here, and I want to make sure he is ok."

"He? Tell me more. He must be pretty special to you for you to track him down." Her mother gives her a knowing look.

"Well, he is intriguing, but I don't want to put the cart before the horse." Dylan says cryptically.

"I know that look, young lady. It looks like you have been bitten by the love bug."

"Mom! Stop!" Dylan laughs while trying to hide the blush creeping up her face.

"Ok, ok, ok. A mother knows when to stop prying. I do want to meet him at some point young lady."

"If there is anything there, yes, you and dad will meet him."

"Ok, thank you for the help. Can you go tell your father that dinner will be ready at 5. He is in the barn and always loses track of time out there."

"Yes, I will" Dylan says while she washes her hands and heads out the door towards the barn.

On her way to the barn, Dylan stopped at the horse corral and Daisy came trotting up. Daisy nuzzled into Dylan as she ran her finger through Daisy's hair. Dylan promises to take her out for a ride after dinner, gives her a pat and continues on to the barn.

Dylan opens the barn door and finds her dad using a grinder on the tractor. Not wanting to disturb him while he is grinding, she stands there and watches until he stops.

"Hey Dad, what's wrong with the tractor?"

"Hey Dilly Bear, it is great to see you again. This part is so rusted on, my only option is to cut it off so I can replace it."

"Ahh ok. Mom wanted me to tell you dinner will be ready at five."

"Sounds good. How are things with you?"

The question asked is not the real question. Dylan knows he is really asking why she is back so soon. She really should make more of an effort to come back regularly.

"I'm trying to find a friend. He is a firefighter in Blue River. He had a bad accident at work and left to work some things out with no way to contact him. His coworkers said his family has land up here and that is where he goes to think."

"Sounds serious. You're not one to chase a boy. You must like him.

When can I meet him?"

"He is a friend. I just want to make sure he is ok."

"Ok Dilly Bear. I trust you know what you are doing. You always have."

Dinner was quiet for the first few bites. There is nothing like a home cooked dinner. During dinner there is no talk about Dylan's search. She is peppered with questions about her career and if is still happy living in the city. She talks in detail about her job and how much she loves it. She is adjusting to city life but it is not the same as out here. She misses the slower pace, fresh air, and natural scenery.

When dinner is finished, she helps clean up and wash the dishes right alongside her mom and dad. Country music is playing softly in the background. The three of them are singing along and washing dishes when her parents suddenly stop and start dancing. The song playing is "I cross my heart" by George Strait. Dylan stops and watches them while the song plays, feeling a sense of longing. She wishes she had someone to do that with. When the song was over, her dad explains that it was their wedding song, and he wanted to dance with his bride again.

With the dishes finished, Dylan heads out towards the corral to take Daisy for a ride before she goes into the stable for the night. Arriving at the barn, she grabs her saddle and then walks to the corral. Daisy sees her coming and trots over. Dylan saddles Daisy and double checks to make sure everything is just right. She then climbs up and they start heading down a trail at a leisurely pace. While walking the trail, Dylan strokes Daisy's neck and mane while talking about her fears, hopes and dreams with regards to Hardy. Daisy answers with a neigh occasionally and Dylan takes that as a good sign.

They continue walking up to the top of a hill to watch the sunset.  Up at the top watching the sun go down, Dylans finds a sense of peace and calm.  She wonders if Hardy is watching the sunset as well.  She feels a little closer to him knowing he is out there somewhere close.  With daylight fading fast, Dylan and Daisy make their way back home.

# 15

Dylan wakes up to the smell of bacon and coffee. She gets up and jumps in the shower. She has a busy day ahead of her. Dressed, she goes downstairs and gives her mom a peck on the cheek and a hug. She sits down and fills her plate with bacon, scrambled eggs, a pancake and some hashbrowns. Her mom sets a glass of orange juice down in front of her along with a mug of coffee.

"This is so good mom. I miss your breakfast buffet." She says in between bites. She finishes her orange juice and then finishes her plate. She doesn't ask about dad. She already knows he has been tending to the animals. He will be in shortly to eat, once the animals have been fed.

Cleaning her place at the table and washing her dishes, she fills a to go cup of coffee and heads out to her car. The first stop is the library. They have a lot of paper records on microfiche. She decides to start there.

Arriving at the library, she parks her car and heads in. The librarian greets her.

"Hello dear, is there anything I can help you with?"

"Yes, I was wondering if you have any county landowner information on microfiche?"

"Yes, we do. I can bring you over to the section. Wait. Dylan Arkham is that you?"

"Yes, it is. Mrs. Abrahamson is that you?"

"Yes dear, it is me."

"When did you start working here? You used to be the school librarian."

"I retired five years ago and was going stir crazy so I volunteer my time here three days a week."

"Wow, good for you."

"Here we are. This section has all the government documents on microfiche for the surrounding counties. I'll be right over there if there is anything else you need."

"Thank you so much."

Dylan looks through the collection and finds several that look promising. She puts the slides in the machine and scrolls through them. After 3 hours of looking at microfiche, she is unable to find any documents highlighting land owned by anyone with the last name Morrison. Feeling dejected, she heads over to the cafe in town for lunch before heading over to the County Clerk's office.

Finding a booth in the corner she sits down and stares out the window. This is turning out to be harder than she thought. As she continues to stare out the window plotting her next move, she hears a voice from her past.

"Dylan Arkham is that you?" a high-pitched squeaky voice says. Dylan turns and sees an older version of her high school friend Mindy standing at her table holding a menu and glass of water.

"Mindy is that you?"

"The one and only. What are you doing here? The last I heard, you had some corporate job in the big city"

"Close. I am an architect in Blue River, Wyoming. I am back visiting my parents. How about you? What have you been up to?"

"Well, Joe and I married right after high school. He owns his own mechanic's garage. I work here part time on the weekends. I have 3 little ones with number four on the way!" Mindy beams while holding her baby bump. "How about you? Got yourself a husband yet?"

"No, no husband. I've been too busy with school and work."

"It looks to me like we both found our happy ever after that we wanted after high school. You were always the one with the dream of college and architecture. I'm glad you followed your dreams. What can I get for you?"

"Chef salad with blue cheese dressing and an iced tea. Thank you"

Mindy brought her meal back and they chatted some more for a bit. Dylan thought it was nice to reconnect with Mindy. She always had the desire to marry Joe and raise a family. She was truly happy for her. It just wasn't the life she wanted. Then she thinks about Hardy and how those thoughts are slowly starting to change.

Dylan finishes her meal and leaves a generous tip for her old friend.

Getting in her car, she heads to the County Clerk's office. The employee was helpful and kind, but again no luck on any land owned by the Morrison family. Feeling down on her luck, she heads back home to the ranch to think.

Arriving back home, she walks in the house, and her mom wraps her up in a hug.

"Thanks for the hug, but what is it for?"

"A mother always knows when their child needs a hug. You looked like you needed a hug."

"Thanks. I couldn't find any records for any land owned by the Morrison family. I've hit a dead end."

"Did you say Morrison?"

"Yeah, why?"

"There is a large chunk of land that the Riley family owned. They put it in a family trust and if I'm not mistaken, their only daughter married. I want to say she married a Morrison. I know it started with an M."

"Really? Are you sure?"

"I'm pretty sure it was Morrison."

"Thanks mom, that is really helpful. I will check on the last name Riley tomorrow."

Dylan spends the rest of the afternoon and early evening helping her dad muck out the stables. They worked in comfortable silence, and she felt good helping her parents out with the ranch chores. She made another mental note to come back more and help. Her parents are aging and this afternoon it was evident that her dad's pace had slowed down. He is still able to do the work; it just takes longer to finish tasks.

With the last stall nearly finished, her mom entered the barn to let them know dinner was ready. After picking up the equipment, they washed up and headed to the house. Dinner was roasted chicken, potatoes, carrots and a salad.

"Dear, do you remember the Riley's?" Her mom asked her dad.

"Yes, why do you ask?"

"They had a daughter who married. Do you remember the last name of the family she married into?"

"I remember her getting married. I know it started with an M. Morrie, Marryington, something like that. Why?"

"Dylan is trying to find land tied to a friend and isn't having much luck. Her friend's last name is Morrison. Could that be it?"

"Yes! Morrison. That is the name!"

"Dilly Bear, if I'm not mistaken, that land is only about 15 miles west of here. I'm not sure of the exact location but there should be records of the Riley's. They have been around for generations."

"Thanks dad, that's where I will start my search tomorrow."

The next morning, Dylan was at the County Clerk office when they opened. The last name Riley was a success. She was able to obtain a copy of the plat map that outlined the property border. Next, she went back to the library and searched for the microfiche files. After several hours of searching, she found a newspaper article announcing the wedding of their daughter to a young man with the last name Morrison. Smiling at herself, she put the microfiche files back and packed up her bag. Things are starting to line up. She can do the rest from home. Her next plan is to merge old with new. She is going to take the plat map and pull up a satellite view of the area on the internet. She can then get an overhead view of the terrain. Treavor said Hardy was building a cabin. She knows it will need to be near a water source, on a flat area of ground, as well as near a fuel source for heat (trees). Hopefully, she can identify an area or two that would be most likely.

She heads back home listening to the music as her excitement builds. She stops at a grocery store on the way home and gathers some supplies she is going to need. She buys jerky, trail mix, and protein bars. She doesn't plan on being out for days, but it is always good to be prepared.

Arriving back home she sets her supplies down on the counter and grabs her computer. She pulls up her internet browser and zooms in on an area identified by the plat map. She spends a couple hours committing the aerial view to memory. She has identified three areas that are possible. There is one area that looks like the best possibility. That is where she will start.

She closes her computer content with her plan. She spends the rest of the day helping her parents. She lets them know of her plan and her anticipated return time. Her parents are initially apprehensive but understand. They trust her judgement and know that she can take care of herself. Her dad insists that she take his truck and not her car. Dylan gives her dad a hug and tries to hide the tears coming down her face. She is thankful for their support and couldn't ask for better parents. She lets them know she will head out in the morning.

# 16

I stand back and admire my work. It has been fun but physically exhausting. The cabin is almost finished. I have just a little bit left on the roof. Eventually, I would like to put a wood burning stove in it but that is a project for another time. I have enjoyed my time sleeping under the stars but must admit it will be nice having an actual roof over my head for the rainy nights.

I am checking the gaps between the wood logs. I have made my own homemade filler by using prairie grass and clay and water. It is not as permanent as cement, however, it is an acceptable substitute. It will require regular maintenance, but it is enough to keep the wind and rain out. I have cut a couple of rough openings to place a couple of windows. Again, another project for another time.

I get started on making a bed frame.  It will be nice to be elevated off the ground.  The last couple of nights it has rained, and my sleeping bag has been a little damp.  Along with the bed, I also want to make a chair and a small table.  The only thing I miss out here (besides Dylan) is listening to music.

That thought causes me to pause and stop what I am doing.  Did I really just admit I miss Dylan? Yes, I did.  It hits me like a punch to the gut.  Maybe I should make two chairs.  One for me and one for Dylan. I smile as I think about this being our little oasis.  That is if she wants to pursue a relationship.  She has told me point blank there is something there, but I am fearful the fire may have changed that.  I add that to my mental list to tackle when I get back.  These last couple weeks with my thoughts have confirmed I do want to go back to the fire department.  I can't think of a better job than that, even with the risks.

I have a week left before I need to be back at work. I will spend the next few days building the smaller items that will make this a little more comfortable.  For the first time, I am excited about my future and look forward to what's to come.  I look up at the sky and send up a prayer of thanks to God that I am still alive.  With my prayer sent, I get back to work building chairs and a table.

Dylan turns off the main road and heads down a dirt road for a little way. She stops the truck and grabs her backpack. She pulls out the plat map and her compass. She identifies her heading and starts walking. She is mesmerized by the beauty of the land. She looks around and sees all the wildlife. She knows she is technically trespassing. She also knows that most ranchers and landowners don't mind backpackers as long as they don't go near livestock or damage the land in any way.

She keeps walking to her landmarks and checks her compass. She estimates about another hour and a half to the first area. She stops, takes out her water bottle and takes a drink. Even if the first area is not correct there is a stream she can use to refill her water bottle.

She decides to sit down and watch the area. If she sits and observes for a while she might see smoke from a fire. If he has been out here this long, he should have a fire going for both cooking and heat at night. She sits and rests with her back against a tree just watching and scanning. She also loves watching the wildlife return when they feel there is no threat to them. She watches turkeys strut by, squirrels romp around, and the occasional deer wander by while grazing. The one thing she did not see? Smoke from a campfire.

She gets up, puts her backpack back on, checks her heading on her compass and identifies a landmark to head towards. She repeats that sequence: Check compass, identify landmark, walk to landmark and repeat. After an hour she reaches the target area. She doesn't immediately see anything. She sets her backpack down by a large tree and walks over to the stream to refill her water bottle. She is slightly disappointed. She thought this was the most promising location. Unfortunately, this location was in the middle of the other two. She has a choice to make, east or west. She only has enough daylight to make it to one more location. If she picks wrong, she will spend the night there and trek to the other location in the morning.

She takes her time here to ensure her water bottle is full. She also eats some of her jerky and trail mix. She sits up against a tree and watches the horizon. Maybe she can see smoke in the sky and that will guide her decision.

She is scanning when she hears a splashing sound and sees movement in her peripheral vision. She looks over to see a trout jumping out of the water and landing with a large splash. She takes a few moments to watch the show of trout jumping out of the water and landing with a splash. She starts laughing and clapping. It felt like a personal show just for her.

After another hour of watching the wildlife and looking for smoke, she decides to head west. She stands up and puts her backpack on. She checks her compass, identifies a landmark and heads out.

After another hour of walking, she arrives at her destination. It looks like she has struck out again. Letting out a frustrated sigh, she starts unpacking. It looks like she is spending the night here. She builds a small fire and grabs her small fishing rod. After about 30 minutes of fishing, she catches a small trout. She cuts the filets off the fish and uses a couple of sticks to hold the meat over the fire to cook.

As she sits down next to the fire, she reflects on the past few months and how much has changed. If she is being honest, her life was becoming dull and stale. She misses this. Hiking through nature, foraging/ hunting/ fishing for food, sleeping under the stars. As much as she was thinking she was going to be there to help Hardy, in a roundabout way, this whole situation has also helped her realize what she is missing. With a sigh of content, she grabs one filet and starts to eat. Fresh trout is actually really good. Cooked over an open fire brings out the flavor.

Before daylight comes to a close, she looks at the plat map and estimates she has a three-hour walk to the last location. If she strikes out there then she will head back home and continue her research and check in with Trevor. Climbing into her sleeping bag, she gazes up at the stars wondering if Hardy is also looking at them. She sees a shooting star and makes a silent wish.

I finish my meal while sitting on the chair that I had built. It is nice to sit on a chair and eat at a table. I feel a sense of accomplishment at making this cabin feel more like home. I have my sleeping bag laid out on the bed frame. I clean the dishes and decide to go for a stroll before I crawl into bed. I head up a small hill to watch the sunset. I make it to the top of the hill and sit down. I can see quite a way from here. I see pronghorn in the distance making their way to bed down for the night. I also see whitetail deer moving through. I look up in the sky and see a bald eagle soaring. I feel a sense of peace and contentment as the sun sinks below the horizon, and the stars light up the sky. I look up and see a shooting star. I make a wish and close my eyes. I start making my way down the hill and back to camp. When I reach camp, I feel energized and unable to sleep. I grab the chair and bring it out of the cabin; I then rummage around my backpack and find the book I brought. Tonight, I am going to treat myself and read a book by the fire.

I read for a while, place a log on the fire and go back to reading. I am not sure how long I have read as I don't have a phone or watch. Feeling tired, I bring the chair back in the cabin, close and lock the door. I curl into my sleeping bag and promptly fall asleep.

Dylan wakes up before the sun has even risen. Excited to start her day, she packs up and extinguishes her campfire. The moon is bright enough that she can identify landmarks and see her compass. She heads off towards her last target area.

She moves quickly in the cool predawn time. Identifying landmarks in the dark is a little more difficult but she is able to do it. She decides to follow close to the river to make travel easier. After a couple hours of walking, her nose picks up on the familiar scent of a campfire. Her heart starts to race and she just knows she is getting close. Her pace picks up as well. She is excited to see him again.

She rounds a riverbend and stops dead in her tracks. She sees a small campfire about 200 feet away with a primitive lean-to. The lean-to looks empty as she scans the area letting her eyes adjust, then she sees it. A black silhouette against a black sky. There is a door that is closed. She decides to sit down in the tree line and wait until sunrise. She doesn't want to surprise whoever is in there while it is dark out, especially if the occupant is not Hardy.  She knows someone is in there because the fire is still going.  Leaning against the tree she closes her eyes listening to the sounds of nature and feels herself starting to nod off to sleep.

I awakened and look around the field of mist. Oh no! Not again. I'm in my nightmare but something feels different.  There is no screaming voice.  I look around and see nothing but fog.  I also don't hear anything.

"Hello?" I call out to the fog. I start to wander unsure of where to go.

"Is anyone out there?" I call out again.

"Hardy, come here" a voice calls out.  It sounds a lot like Mary. I miss the sound of the voice and start crying.

"It's ok Hardy. Don't cry.  We are over here."  I start walking towards the voice.

"Who's we? What do you want?"

"It is us Hardy. Mary, Wilma, and Theo."  Suddenly, I see them appear from the fog.  My little babies are running to me, arms wide open with huge smiles on their faces.

"Daddy, Daddy, Daddy" they yell out as they run into my arms. I wrap them up in a big hug and kiss their heads.  I don't care if this is a dream.  I am going to soak up every moment of this.

"Hello Hardy. We miss you. Please stop punishing yourself. The fire wasn't your fault. You need to live your life. We are in a good place now." Mary says as she looks me in the eye. I stand up and wrap her in a big hug.

"I miss you guys so much. I feel empty without you." I say through a choking sob.

"We know. It has been heartbreaking to watch you punish yourself over an accident. Please stop. We will meet again when the time is right. You need to let her in, Hardy. She is a good soul. We must be going now. Our time in this realm is limited."

"NO, we just got here. Please don't go. Please don't" I choke out through the tears.

"Bye daddy. See you later. I love you" both my babies say together.

"Hardy, know that we always love you but don't push her away. Opportunity is knocking on your door. You need to open the door, Hardy. Opportunity is knocking" Mary says as she and the kids fade away back into the fog.

KNOCK, KNOCK, KNOCK, KNOCK

I open my eyes and look around the cabin. What a weird dream. Pleasant but weird.

KNOCK, KNOCK, KNOCK, KNOCK

I bolt upright. Something is knocking at the door. I jump out of my sleeping bag and throw on my clothes. I grab my knife and cautiously go to the door. I slide the lock open and slowly open the door. I blink a couple of times without believing what I am seeing.

"Dylan? Is that really you?" I sputter in shock.

"Hi Hardy." Dylan says a blush creeping up your face. "You're probably wondering why I am here huh"

"Um yeah, among other things." I say still shaking the cobwebs out of my brain.

"See, the thing is you left without saying goodbye or when you would be back. These last few weeks have been horrible. I didn't know how you were doing, if you were ok, and then it hit me. I love you, Hardy Morrison. You have awoken something inside of me that I didn't know I was missing. I asked around and Trevor told me about this land. So, I came to find you. I couldn't wait. If you don't want me around or to see where this can go fine. But I need to hear it from you before I can walk away, as difficult as that would be."

I stare at her, unable to speak. She loves me? Even with everything that has happened, she went to all this trouble to find me and tell me she loves me?

"Well... Can you say something? Anything?" Dylan says, staring at me.

"I'm sorry. You have caught me off guard. Please come in. We need to chat." I say as I hold the door open and move to the side to make room.

"I told you I have a history and my family died. Well, if we are going to explore whatever this is." I motion between the two of us "then you need to hear everything."

"OK, I'm listening Hardy"

"My wife's name is Mary. Then there is Wilma who was three and

Theo who was one. I was at work one night. I worked as a paramedic for Lime County EMS. We were stationed on the other side of the county when I heard the call come out. Blue River Fire and Lime County EMS were dispatched for a house fire. It was called in by someone driving by. I started driving to the call when dispatch told us to stand down. I couldn't. Trevor was my partner, and he knew I just had to get there. If I could get there quick enough, maybe I could save them."

I hear Dylan gasp.

"When we arrived, no one was going inside the house. There was fire coming out of every window. I saw a firefighter on the back of the truck crying. I lost it. I started screaming and crying. They were dead. I read the fire report. Lightning had struck a tree, and a branch came down on the power lines. The power lines were still live when they disconnected from the house and that started the shrubs on fire. The fire engulfed the propane tanks I had next to the grill next to the house. They were old tanks and did not have a relief valve. I had meant to change them out, just never got around to it. The tanks heated to the point they Bleve'd. It just so happened that when the tanks Bleve'd and shattered the sliding glass door, the wind was pushing the fire inside the house. It was a wind-driven fire and it blocked the stairs. The bedroom door and window were open. The investigator thinks Mary saw their only option was to go out the window. When she opened the window without shutting the bedroom door it created a flow path of smoke, heat, and fire."

I heard another gasp from Dylan, but she hasn't said anything.

"They were found huddled together just below the window on the ground.  The Medical Examiner thinks they died of carbon monoxide poisoning before the flames reached them.  I sure hope that is the case. I held it together until the funeral.  After the funeral, I spiraled out of control with heavy drinking and depression.  I quit my job and shut everyone out of my life.  I blamed myself because if I hadn't stored the propane tanks there or had switched them out with ones that had a relief valve, they probably would have had a chance to escape."

"Hardy, it wasn't your fault."

"I realize that now, but it took me a long time and a lot of help to get to this place.  My drinking was so out of control I passed out on my front lawn.  My neighbor called 911. I had to go to court. I could see pity in the eyes of everyone.  They felt sorry for me.  It pissed me off even more. I was ordered to complete community service.  I did my community service working in landscaping.  After my time was completed, I stayed on and worked for the company.  I also was ordered to go to therapy. Between my therapist and the landscaping job I was improving a little bit, but I had these awful nightmares where my wife was yelling at me that it was all my fault."

"Oh Hardy. You also had Trevor."

"No, he tried to stay in contact, but I kept shutting him out.  We recently reconnected after I took the job with the fire department. My therapist was excited that I had applied.  It was a huge step in the right direction.  Manny, my landscaping boss, was also relieved.  He liked having me on his crew but knew I needed to get back to being a paramedic. Fast forward a little bit, then you come into my life. Before we officially met, I kept seeing your vibrant emerald green eyes.  They drew me in like a magnet. I couldn't look away. I vowed to never get involved with anyone ever again because of the hurt and pain of losing them but you have covertly taken down those walls I have put up. Last night I had a dream. It was my family saying they are ok, and I need to live my life and that it wasn't my fault. Mary told me to let her in. Those were her exact words… let her in. I think she was referring to you. Then, this is the freaky part. As they were fading back into the fog, she said opportunity is knocking and that I need to open the door. When I woke up, you were knocking on my door"

"Oh Hardy, I am so sorry you went through that. I am here and will be for as long as you'll let me be. I want to walk through the rest of this journey with you. Will you let me?"

"How can I say no to the two women that I have loved? Yes, you heard that right. I love you, Dylan Arkham. I came to that realization while I was out here alone wishing you were here with me. And now you're here."

We spend the morning lying on my bed in the cabin and chatting about her adventure finding me. I am amazed at the resilience and dedication she displayed. It helps push me to be more resilient in the struggles that I face. When both of our stomachs rumble, we go out to the river and catch some fish. Over breakfast we talk about the cabin and how I built it by myself.

We decide to spend a few days out here just the two of us to get to know each other better. She continues to amaze me with her wilderness survival knowledge and abilities, and I know I made the right decision to let her into my heart.

"So Hardy, what would you say to meeting my parents?  I know this is new, but they live 20 minutes away from here and it was my homebase while I searched for you. My suitcase and car are still there.  My dad insisted I take his truck out here."

"I would love to meet the parents who raised such an independent and tough woman such as yourself."

We finish packing up the campsite and start hiking back out to my truck, when I realized I don't know where she parked.

"Where are you parked?" I asked her

"I parked southeast of here.  Where did you park?"

"The same" I said with a smile.  Yep, we were meant for each other.

We walk a few hours and reach my truck. I don't see her truck.  She sees my confused look.

"Oh, I didn't drive this far down the road.  I am closer to the main road."

We load up everything into my truck and I drive down to hers.  She jumps out and gets in her vehicle.  She turns around and I follow her to her parents place.

We arrive at her parents' ranch and I am impressed and jealous at the same time.  This is where she grew up? No wonder she is as strong and independent as she is.  I see a woman who I assume is her mother come out of the house and approach.  Wiping my sweaty palms on my pants I get out of the truck and approach. Dylan gives her mom a huge hug. Her mom then turns to me.

"And whom do I have the pleasure of meeting?"

"Hardy Morrison ma'am. Pleased to meet you." I reach out to shake her hand and she brings me in for a hug.

"You take good care of her; I can tell she is head over heels for you. About time if you ask me." She says with a wink.

"I don't believe she needs to be taken care of, but I will be with her every step of the way through life." I say with a smile towards Dylan. I grab her hand and bring her in for a hug.

I hear a throat clear behind me.

"Son, it isn't proper to hug a lady in front of her father before introducing yourself." I hear a gruff male voice say behind me.

"Oh dad, stop it." I hear Dylan reply.

"Hi Dilly Bear. I'm glad you're home." I give Dylan a smirk and she gives me a look that tells me to keep quiet. I try to hide my laugh.

"Sir, nice to meet you. I'm Hardy Morrison. "

"Nice to meet you. Are you opposed to hard work?"

"No sir, not at all."

"Ok, then. Can you give me a hand?"

"Absolutely"

Mr. Arkham and I go to the barn, and I help him with menial tasks and repairs. He questions me further while we work and I feel like I passed his test. Dyan and I spend the rest of the day helping on the ranch. Her mom made one of the best home cooked meals I had ever had. I felt truly blessed. Dylan showed me her old room and helped make up the guest bedroom for me. We took a walk that evening to watch the sunset. On the top of a small hill, we watched the sun sink down below the horizon. When the stars came out, we shared our first kiss, and it was magical. I never wanted it to end. We returned to the house and headed off to our separate rooms.

The next morning, I woke up to the smell of coffee and bacon. I showered and dressed and made my way down the stairs. Dylan was chatting with her mom while loading up her plate. I joined in and filled a plate. My first cup of non-cowboy coffee was delicious and amazing. After breakfast we helped clean up and loaded our vehicles. I wish we could make the journey back in one car, but it just isn't possible. We stop for lunch after a couple hours of driving before hitting the road again.

As I pull into town, a realization hit me. I love her, she loves me. Life is short, why wait. The fourth of July is coming up in a few days. When I first saw her emerald green eyes there were fireworks. What better time to propose than on the fourth of July during the fireworks. It is a good thing I already spoke with her father. Not that she needs his permission, she is an adult and can make her own choice, but he did give me his blessing for when the time is right. That time is now. I know just the jewelry store to go to. I will find the perfect ring for Dylan.

# ABOUT THE AUTHOR

The author lives in the upper Midwest with his wife, kids, dog, and bird.  He has been working in public safety since 2002.  When not working or writing, he enjoys hiking, hunting, fishing, camping, kayaking, and golfing.  He took a creative writing course during his sophomore year of college and after twenty plus years, has finally decided to make time to write books.

Connect with the Author on the following platforms:

Pintrist: ekubatcreativewriting

Instagram: erickubatcreativewriting

Facebook: Eric Kubat creative writing group page

Goodreads: Eric Kubat

Email: eric.kubat.creativewriting@gmail.com